Coffee with a Superhero

Cleo Burwood

Contents

Chapter 1
Lucy

My first coffee of the day splashed everywhere when I tried to answer my cell phone. I was walking through the streets of the Upper West Side in New York, heading to work, and the reusable travel cup tilted sideways in my hand as I hunted for the phone squealing insistently inside my satchel style briefcase.

Noting the call was from an unknown number, I answered professionally, "Hello, this is Lucia Cortez." Not quite so professionally, though, there was coffee dripping down my hand and arm as I pressed the phone against my ear.

A very polite women at the other end of the call said, "Dr Cortez, this is the White House operator, please hold for Oran Coombes, Chief of Staff."

I sucked in a breath, my thoughts racing. The White House? Why was the White House Chief of Staff calling me first thing on a Monday morning?

The call connected before I managed to get my thoughts in order. "Dr Cortez, good morning. This is Oran

Coombes from the White House. Are you somewhere you can talk for a moment?"

It was a crisp clear spring morning, and the street was full of locals starting their week and tourists heading out of their hotels for a packed day of sightseeing. There was plenty of background noise, but apart from the dripping coffee I could manage.

"Good morning, Mr Coombes. I am on a busy sidewalk in New York but happy to talk, how can I help?"

"Let me get straight to the point. The President has asked that you join her at a meeting later today. President Clifton is gathering a group of scientist for an emergency taskforce that will meet for at least the next few days. She would like you to be part of that group."

"Today?" I clarified, my voice shaking slightly as I strained to keep the incredulous tone under control. How was I going to reorganise my week to spend it in Washington?

"That's right. 4pm today at the White House. I will organise a staffer to assist you with getting a flight to Washington."

"Thank you, that would be helpful. But may I ask what I should do when I get there? Where do I go?"

"My assistant will email you with all the details, including instructions about security and where to go when you arrive. We will arrange the flights and hotel accommodation for you. Please bring clothes and other things you need for a stay of a few days."

"And finally," Oran continued, "this matter is extremely confidential, so you must not tell anyone you are coming to the White House today. I have several other calls to make, so thank you Dr Cortez. I will see you this afternoon."

With that he ended the call. I stood quietly for a

moment clutching the remainder of my spilled coffee, while my mind caught up with what had just happened. It seemed I was now on my way to Washington. It was currently just before 9am so I had seven hours to reorganise my week, go home and pack some clothes, get on a flight and be at the White House ready for a meeting with the President. While I had long admired President Clifton I was slightly overwhelmed that I would now have the opportunity to meet her in person.

Today my workday was supposed to have been spent on campus at Endeavour University, progressing my various research projects and supervising my graduate students. As I didn't have a formal teaching role at the university there were no classes that would need to be covered while I was in Washington, but there was still a lot of juggling required for me to be unexpectedly out of town for a few days.

The next few hours were a blur, and neither my heart nor my thoughts would stop racing until I got to the airline lounge at La Guardia Airport shortly before noon. I had headed home straight after the phone call and spoken to an assistant at the White House to organise a flight and car service. I then contacted my students, the heads of department at both universities where I worked, and finally my parents to let them all know I was going out of town for a few days.

I had made it into central Washington easily from the airport, so by 3.45pm I was in the foyer of the White House, ready and waiting for my 4pm meeting. My suitcase was waiting for me in the White House security office.

Washington was generally familiar to me, as I had

attended various meetings and conferences there over the years, but I had never been to the White House. The security guard had directed me to a small waiting area with red velvet chairs around the walls. I sat in that room for a few minutes trying to look calm and professional on the outside, hiding signs of my anxiety. My body and my mind were feeling stage fright, as if I was about to sit a university exam or do a job interview.

I took a few deep breaths and closed my eyes for a just a moment but then jumped at the sound of someone calling my name. "Dr Cortez, come with me please."

A friendly woman who introduced herself as Mary asked me to follow her, and together we walked very quickly through the corridors. We paused for a moment in an office area, and then I was ushered into the Oval Office.

President Clifton stood in front of the Resolute desk, talking with a group of several people. About five or six more were seated on the couches and armchairs in the room. The President turned as the door opened and smiled as I was announced by Mary, "Dr Lucia Cortez, Madam President, from Endeavour University and Logan Technology Institute."

"Welcome Dr Cortez, please join us," President Clifton sounded exactly like she did on the TV, with her tone warm but commanding. A legend to many Americans my age, she was the women who had finally broken the highest glass ceiling in the world when she was elected President three years ago. Tara Clifton was a tall woman in her early 60s whose bearing hinted at the fact that she had been in the military for much of her life, serving as an Air Force lawyer. She had entered politics about 10 years ago when she ran for Senator for her home state.

"Good afternoon, Ma'am," I said, trying to keep my voice calm and remembering to breathe.

The President smiled again and waved me towards the couches to take a seat. These were the famous Oval Office couches that faced each other across the Presidential Seal in the carpet. I had watched so many movies and political TV shows where critical conversations had happened in this room.

As I sat down an older gentleman came towards me with a hand outstretched in introduction. "Oran Coombes, Dr Cortez. We spoke this morning." He had a short salt and pepper beard and thick glasses, which framed a set of very tired looking green eyes.

"It's nice to meet you Mr Coombes." I said formally.

One of the other men gathered with the President spoke. "Just one more external visitor, Ma'am and we can then get started. Let's do introductions when everyone is here." I thought he might be the National Security Advisor, Ben Isaacs, but I wasn't sure.

The Oval Office door opened again and in walked someone I definitely did recognise. Mary the staffer announced this visitor with a smile, her professional demeanour slipping just a little, "Mr Cyran, Madam President, from the United Nations, and also from the planet JandaKo."

The man who came through the door and strode confidently into the Oval Office was probably the most famous person on the planet, with far more name recognition than the President herself. As Earth's only known extraterrestrial alien, and someone who had a very public role, Cyran was well known across the globe.

He was a little over six feet tall, and looked basically human except for his eyes, which were the colour of vibrant copper with multiple flecks of gold. He had long dark blonde hair that fell in waves down just past his shoulders. Cyran was dressed as he always was in a grey-greenish uniform style flight suit and matching boots. Both were apparently made from a material that had a leather like appearance, but which I understood from news articles was a heat and pressure resistant synthetic material made from alien technology.

"Good afternoon, Madam President," he said politely with a smile as he walked forward and offered his hand to her. "Apologies if I kept you waiting." Cyran's voice was warm and rich, with just a trace of an English accent. Cyran turned his attention to the others in the room. "Hello everyone."

Reassuring Cyran that he was not late, President Clifton waved him towards a chair, as she had done to me. Cyran turned towards where I was sitting at one end of the couch but did not take the vacant spot to my right. Instead, he took one of the wing-backed chairs, so he was sitting on my left, directly next to the President's chair at the top of the couches. As he sat, Cyran turned towards me and offered a brief hello. I smiled at him, a little shocked that my day, which had started so ordinarily in New York, had ended up with me meeting an alien in the Oval Office.

Most of the world knew Cyran's backstory. It had a been an international sensation when the spaceship carrying him and his family had suddenly landed at Stonehenge on a one rainy October afternoon nearly 25 years ago. Two questions were answered that day, the big one of whether we were alone in the universe and also why Stonehenge had been built. It was a marker for a safe landing place for ships of an alien race who had last visited Earth 5000 years ago.

The footage of the landing was iconic, as were the first dramatic scenes of the British military and scientists venturing into the ship. Sadly though, they quickly determined that Cyran's family had all died in their stasis pods during the journey and he was the only one still breathing and able to be revived.

No-one had been able to determine exactly how long the family had been traveling, or why Cyran was the sole survivor. He was the youngest of the family at only about eight years old, with his four siblings all older, so possibly it was because he was the youngest.

For the first five years after his arrival, Cyran had been constantly in the news, with governments and scientists across the world vying for the chance to study him and his ship's technology. It became obvious very quickly that while he looked mostly human, except for his eyes, he had a strength and speed well beyond that of an ordinary human child.

Then Cyran had disappeared from the public eye, with the British Government only saying that he was being given some space to experience Earth culture and his teenage years in private. Many conspiracy theories abounded to fill the void of news about Cyran, about how he had been sent home, or killed by the CIA, or that the spaceship landing had always been a hoax.

Eight years ago, however, the Secretary General of the United Nations had announced that Cyran was going to be actively working for the UN as a Special Disaster Response Envoy, using his super strength and speed to assist first responders with saving people when natural disasters or accidents happened. That fancy job title hadn't really stuck, and first the world's media and then everyone else had just started referring to Cyran as a superhero.

There was no time for me to properly speak to Cyran, as President Clifton quickly called the meeting to order. She shared with us some disturbing news, outlining that NASA had identified that in September, Earth was going to have a very close call with a small previously unknown comet. The comet was officially known as the Mauna Kea comet, after the observatory in Hawaii where it had been first observed.

"I am told modelling is so tight that we will not know the comet's final trajectory until it is very close to Earth," the President explained. "So, we need to plan for the worst outcome and hope for the best. The best would be Earth passing through the tail of the comet and us all getting a spectacular meteor shower. However, the worst would be an impact from the comet, and we need to take whatever steps we can to reduce that threat. As such, an emergency taskforce is being set up. The taskforce will comprise of everyone here, plus other scientists from space agencies and universities around the globe, and military personnel and NASA staff. Given it is now the end of April, we have four months before the comet arrives to develop and implement a solution."

President Clifton turned slightly so she was looking directly at Cyran. "Cyran will be working with the task-force in a diplomatic capacity as a representative of the United Nations and will also be able to provide help with his unique physical skillset if needed. Thank you for that Cyran." Beside me, Cyran nodded to acknowledge her words.

The President continued, "I have spoken extensively to the Secretary General of the United Nations and to a range of world leaders about this issue over the last few days. Everyone agrees that secrecy is appropriate in the short term until we have more information. This means we will not be telling the public for several months yet."

Everyone was quiet, processing the implications of what we had just been told. Oran Coombes took over from the President, telling us the taskforce would officially start meeting at 8am the following morning at NASA's headquarters here in Washington, and that we would meet every day until there was a suitable resolution. Hotel accommodation would be provided nearby for the duration.

The President stood up and walked to her desk, signalling the end of the meeting. "I have other things to attend to now but thank you everyone and good luck with your important task."

Chapter 2
Lucy

At 7.30am the following morning I left my uninspiring Washington DC hotel. The hotel was located just over a block from NASA headquarters, so I assumed it had been chosen for its convenience rather than the quality of the beds or facilities. It appeared to cater primarily to government workers, which was not surprising given its location in central Washington. There was a group dressed in FBI windbreakers huddled in one corner of the lobby as I walked through.

Outside on the street it was windy and not anywhere near as warm as it had been yesterday in New York. Arriving at NASA headquarters on E Street, I went through security and then was escorted into a large, bland grey conference room. A U-shaped meeting table filled the room, and the chairs were arranged to face a whiteboard and a large display screen on the side wall which currently had the NASA logo on it. One wall of the room was primarily glass, with full height windows and a set of double doors that led out to a small courtyard area. I saw a few patio chairs and some potted plants outside the doors.

Coffee with a Superhero

There was a sad looking coffee station in one corner of the room, with a half full coffee pot and an urn for hot water. Next to it was table with a large stack of bottled water. After navigating around the table looking at the name plates to find my allocated seat and put my bag down, I headed towards the coffee. There was no real milk or cream, only creamer, and the coffee smelt burnt. No thanks. Regretting I had not stopped for coffee on my way in, I wished a trendy little cafe would suddenly appear in the corner of the room.

The room was already quite full as there was about 25 people who had arrived before me. Most were chatting quietly in small groups, and a few were working on laptops at the meeting room table. There were many people in business attire, some people dressed more casually most of whom were probably scientists, and others were in military uniform. I did not know anyone in the room, and no-one had spoken to me as I walked in.

At 28 years old I was likely to be one of the youngest members of the taskforce. I had considerable experience with being the youngest person in the room in work situations. Unfortunately, I was also used to people, mostly middle-aged men, assuming I was someone's assistant or one of the serving staff.

I was dreading being stuck in this room with all these people for many days. That felt like way too much 'peopling' for me. I could be social and make polite conversation with people I didn't know, but I found it very draining. Give me a small group of people who had similar interests to mine, however, and you could not stop me talking.

Taking off my jacket, I hung it over the back of my chair and sat down at my spot at the meeting table. I was dressed in my 'conference clothes' which were more formal and professional than what I would wear around campus. Today this was black pants, with a red boat neck shirt and a colourful scarf around my neck. Scarves were a great accessory in long meetings, playing with them gave me something to do with my hands and helped with my focus. I had fancy black sneakers on my feet as I could not stand wearing high heeled shoes, and my black jacket was draped over the back of my chair.

The conference room door opened again, swinging inwards. Oran Coombes stepped through and held the door open. Cyran then walked into the room, looking relaxed and confident. He was chatting to a woman I recognised as Sandra Malone the Director of NASA.

It had been a thrill meeting Cyran yesterday even though we had not really spoken other than his casual hello. As he walked in, I wondered briefly where he had spent the night, doubting that it would have been in a Washington hotel. It was common knowledge he had lived in the United Kingdom when he arrived on Earth but given that he could fly quickly around the globe, he could now be living anywhere.

Director Malone strode towards the centre chair at the bottom part of the U-shaped table. She was chairing the taskforce meeting. Oran Coombes took the spot on the Director's right and Cyran the one on her left. Cyran had a smile on his face that was all professional charm, but which didn't seem to be quite genuine. I wondered if like me he too was uncomfortable about being here.

Unsurprisingly, we started with introductions. There were senior officers from all branches of the military, people from various areas in NASA, and representatives from the space agencies of several countries, some of whom were joining via secure video link from their home countries. The scientists included some geologists, a communications specialist and meteorologist.

When it was my turn, I introduced myself, "I am Dr Lucy Cortez, a physicist and engineer. I have academic and research roles at both Endeavour University in New York and the Logan Technology Institute in Boston. I am also a board member at the green energy company Bright Eco-electricity."

The formal part of the morning started with an extensive presentation from the NASA team on everything they knew about the comet. This was followed by several hours of very intense discussion. We had a short break mid-morning for more bad coffee and chocolate chip cookies, and by the time we broke for lunch at 1pm I was very hungry.

About an hour before the lunch break, I had noticed someone entering the conference room pushing a trolley stacked with trays of food and several large carafes of water and orange juice. The food had been set up on a previously empty table near the coffee station.

When I approached the lunch table, I looked with dismay at the limp sandwiches on the trays. They had been sitting out in the warm room for nearly an hour. This sort of food was not my style at all. I had never been a sandwich sort of person and, although I was hungry, the thought of eating anything on that food trolley made my stomach churn.

Heading away from the crowd gathered around the food, I pushed open the glass doors to the courtyard and went outside. It was quiet and peaceful out here. I needed a break away from the intensity of the conversations around the table and having to be 'on' the whole time. Finding a spot behind the large potted plants so I was mostly out of sight, I leaned back against the side wall of the courtyard with my eyes shut and took a few deep breaths.

A few minutes later, I opened my eyes when a deep voice said, "Hello, Dr Cortez, are you okay here?" It was Cyran. He was smiling at me, his face warm and open but with a hint of concern showing in his otherworldly golden eyes. "It's a bit intense in there isn't it?"

I nodded, trying to focus my thoughts. "Hello. Yes, to both of those questions," I managed in response.

Cyran was only holding a bottle of water. Perhaps he was not having lunch either. "I am not stalking you, I promise," he said. "I just noticed you were out here without any food, and I wanted to make sure you were alright."

As Cyran seemed to be genuinely concerned, I decided to be honest about the whole lunch situation. "I hate the sandwiches at these types of things. Who puts all the fillings all in together? There are so many food things I can't tolerate and one of them is limp bread with warm margarine, and so I would rather go hungry than eat that crap...," I blurted out, and then trailed off as I saw him smiling at me and trying not to laugh.

"I see, that sounds like a major problem, Dr Cortez. I apologise on behalf of NASA that there is not a better lunch available." His words sounded formal, but his smile softened his words.

"Sorry for that outburst," I said in a much calmer manner. "I am not normally that annoyed about lunch items, but I was just a bit overwhelmed. Anyway, no need to be quite so formal, my name is Lucia, my friends call me Lucy." I stuck out my hand to Cyran, hoping that was acceptable etiquette. I had never met anyone from another planet before. He took my hand in his much larger one and shook it gently.

"I hope I count as a friend now that you have shared your hatred of sandwiches with me, so may I call you Lucy? And your secret is safe with me." His voice had a warm rich tone as he laughed gently. He did not have a strong accent as he spoke, although he came across as definitely British.

"Of course you can call me Lucy. I think we will definitely have to be friends after you were so gracious about my embarrassing rant. But I notice you are not eating either, is that also some secret sandwich hating thing going on, or is that just a weird alien food thing?"

Thankfully Cyran laughed again rather than taking offence. He leaned in towards me to say conspiratorially, "Not a weird alien food thing. I just tend not to eat at public events, too much danger of getting mustard down the front of me and it spoiling my image by it being on the front page of every newspaper in the world the next day."

"So you're not afraid of a hurricane or a nuclear warhead, but you are afraid of mustard?" I asked jokingly.

"Yep, that's pretty much it." His voice was filled with laughter. "You know my deepest darkest secret. We have to be friends now."

Chapter 3
Cyran

We stood there in the courtyard behind the potted plants smiling at each other and the shared joke, for what must have been only a few seconds, but it felt like many long, amazing minutes.

I was working, so I was supposed to have the mask of my super professional, slightly aloof alien persona in place. I was not supposed to be laughing with sexy American scientists. But it seemed that Dr Cortez, or Lucy as I was now instructed to call her, had managed to melt my mask a little. Here I was discussing sandwiches and talking about mustard with a woman I didn't really know.

I had come out of the meeting room into the open air of the courtyard so I could make a quick trip home. Eating was not the only thing I didn't like to do in public while dressed like this, and I wanted to go home for a very quick bathroom break and to grab some food.

Home for me was a flat in central London. Since age thirteen when I had been able to start to live a relatively normal lifestyle, I had lived in the London area, first with my adoptive Earth family and now by myself. At a relaxed flying speed, it was about a three-minute commute from Washington, or if I rushed, I could be back there in about 90 seconds.

When I had noticed Lucy standing outside all alone, I had felt compelled to check on her. It was obvious she was not a damsel in distress who needed rescuing, but this morning had been hard for all of us. If there was anything I could do to help her endure the taskforce meeting I was happy to do so. While I didn't want to be rude and fly off when we had just started talking, I realised that perhaps I could solve two problems at once.

"I was just about to take off for a few minutes," I explained, making a hand gesture somewhat like a plane taking off. "Perhaps I can get you some real food while I am gone?"

"Oh yes, that would be fabulous." I could hear a mix of both relief and excitement in her voice. "Anything but sandwiches would be great, but preferably something warm. I am generally not a fan of cold food."

"But only if that's okay with you to do that?" Lucy continued. "I don't want to burden you."

"Don't worry. It will be my pleasure. Do you like curry? I know a place that does a great butter chicken." It was my local takeaway place in London. "Given we have only a half hour break, I had better get going, but I will be back in about 15 minutes."

Lucy nodded her agreement. "Thank you that sounds perfect."

Stepping back into the middle of the courtyard, I raised my left hand upward and mentally and physically pushing downwards I leapt into the sky.

It was 14 minutes later that I returned to Washington. I had stopped briefly before I crossed the Atlantic to do an online order for four curry and rice dishes from a restaurant that was very close to my flat. When I arrived home, I changed into normal street clothes, grabbed a pair of sunglasses to hide my eyes, and headed around the corner to get the food.

Back at home, I had put Lucy's lunch in a small, insulated carry bag, and then very quickly ate the other three curry meals. Three large meals were about the right amount to fill me up. I ate an enormous quantity of food each day, particularly if I was burning calories flying regularly between continents.

I had always had a large appetite, but when I started working full time as a superhero, I had needed to dramatically increase the number of calories I was consuming daily. I had found the right balance with an energy intake of about four times what it would be if I was a human.

When I landed in the back in the courtyard at NASA headquarters Lucy was sitting at one of the patio tables, concentrating on typing something on her phone. She looked up as I landed, probably alerted by the rushing of the wind. Handing her the brown paper bag I said with a smile, "Delivery for Dr Lucy."

The glass doors leading out from the meeting room opened and Director Malone walked through into the courtyard. She must have seen me arrive. Coming towards us, she called out, "Cyran, you are back. Do you have a moment?"

Reaching the spot where Lucy and I were standing, the Director lowered her voice and said, "I would like your help in a discussion with the Chinese scientists. I am hoping you can be a neutral party and assist with translations if needed." Then acknowledging Lucy was standing beside me she continued, "Sorry to interrupt Dr Cortez. May I borrow Cyran please?" Duty was calling.

When Director Malone had asked for my help with the Chinese scientists at the lunch break, I was glad to be more usefully involved with the discussions, even though it meant missing out on more of a chance to talk to Lucy. I felt my role on the taskforce was a diplomatic one as much as anything else, particularly in these early planning sessions where the focus was on the scientific details.

Over the last few years, I had sat in a range of high-level international discussions as a neutral representative of the United Nations, and I enjoyed the diplomatic work as well as the physical side of being a superhero. I spoke all the major Earth languages and that greatly increased my ability to connect with leaders and diplomats from across the globe.

Being part of the taskforce meeting today required a very different skill set. I wasn't used to having to sit and listen attentively, waiting around to answer questions about just how strong I was (very) and how long I could hold my breath if working in space (about 15 minutes comfortably, with the longest so far being 22 minutes).

I was not generally comfortable at events where I needed to be 'on' and in character as Cyran the alien super-hero for long periods of time. I preferred flying in somewhere and doing a quick rescue and then going home. Diplomatic events hosted by the United Nations were usually short and sharp international meetings, or the occasional cocktail party where I needed to make small talk with world leaders, rather than long periods of time in the same room.

The fact that I was sitting next to Director Malone at the top of the table made the situation worse, as she was chairing the meeting and everyone was looking in our direction. No hiding in the corner for me.

Lucy was sitting on one of the side arms of the U-shaped table, amongst the other scientists. When she swivelled in her chair to face the screen I could see her in profile. I noticed that often her fingers were playing with the ends of her scarf, and I wondered if she was conscious that she was doing it as she sat and listening intently.

I admired the way Lucy was holding her own in the conversations around the table. Several times during the afternoon she had firmly but politely stated her position on an issue or interjected with a suggested approach or additional fact about what someone was saying. Unfortunately, a few times I had got a vibe from some of the taskforce members, that they were dismissive of Lucy's ideas when she put them forward. I was used to getting treated with a level of respect and deference by the people I worked with, but I imagined that Lucy might have had a somewhat different experience as a relatively young female.

Early in the afternoon my thoughts about Lucy were abruptly interrupted when one of the NASA engineers started discussing my family's spaceship and asked me whether there was a way that the ship could be made viable again for spaceflight. I suppose that from his perspective, he was discussing a piece of technology that could potentially be used to assist get a missile payload into space if needed.

But for me, the ship wasn't just a potential tool to help fight the comet. It was the place where my family had perished all those years ago in the cold of space. My heart started pounding and my breathing grew shallower as a wave of sadness and grief washed through me as my memories came to the front of my mind.

More than 20 years ago I had woken up on my family's spaceship, only about eight years old, to a world that was completely different from everything I had previously known. For me it had felt like a few minutes before that when father had popped me in the stasis pod. He told me it would be just like going to sleep, and then we would all wake up in our new home on the colony planet in a neighbouring solar system to our planet JandaKo.

However, when I did wake up my parents and siblings were all gone, having died during the long voyage. Based on the ship's logs, scientists had estimated it had been a journey of a few hundred Earth years. It seemed that the ship's computer had automatically changed our course after encountering a violent plasma storm and headed towards another habitable planet that was in its database from previous explorations, that being Earth.

I managed to politely answer the NASA engineer's question, reiterating what I knew about the ships power banks being severely deleted during the long flight, and the unavailability of the elements needed to refuel on Earth.

Then on the pretext of getting a drink, I got up from my chair and walked across the room towards the table holding the bottled water. Grabbing a drink, I stood next to the table with my back against the wall, trying to ride the wave of sadness and focus on the now.

I still missed my original family, but most of the time now they felt very distant, and I had a fabulous new Earth family. While I had been well cared for by the authorities when I had arrived on Earth, for the first few years I had been kept away from the community while the scientists and medical personnel tested both me and my ship. They had tried to get me to help them understand the workings of the ship and our technology, but at eight years old I was not an expert in interstellar spaceship technology and there was a lot of frustration all round.

I had learnt English very quickly, and with a few months was fluent in English as well as several other languages spoken by the team who were working with me. After a few years, I started living with the family of one of the linguists on the team named John Harrington. That's when I became Curtis Harrington, a normal English boy with a Mum and Dad and older sister, living in a suburban house in London and eventually attending school. My identity as Cyran the orphan alien became something that I kept hidden.

I had continued to work with the UK Government on understanding my home planet's technology, often spending the school holidays and then later my university breaks working in the large warehouse in central England where the spaceship was housed.

Neither my family nor the Government had been pleased when at 26 years old I had wanted to come out as Cyran and start using my alien abilities to do public rescue work across the globe. My family had wanted to protect me and my secret identity. The Government wanted me to remain their exclusive asset, particularly as Britain had got significant international prestige from my family's ship 'choosing' to land at Stonehenge.

It had felt very wrong to me, however, to go on just pretending I was a normal human and hiding my abilities, when I could help so many people. When I refused to back down the UK Government had begrudgingly supported me and put me in touch with the United

Nations, so I had the protection of being non-political in my work.

The taskforce meeting was continuing as I stood in the corner thinking about my life, so I knew I was time to push aside my sadness, return to my seat and tune back into the conversation. The current topic was something about whether we could combine satellites in low earth orbit to create a deflector array.

I went back to my seat and saw Lucy looking back towards me, with an expression of curiosity and concern. I smiled across at her and gave her a discreet thumbs up to let her know I was all good. I had enjoyed our brief conversations earlier in the day and she seemed very lovely. It had been a pleasure to organise lunch for her, and hopefully I would get a chance to get to know her better in coming days.

The taskforce meeting continued well into the early evening. It was just after 7pm before Director Malone declared us finished for the day, and the relief around the table was palpable. "Let's meet back at 8am tomorrow please," she asked everyone.

The mood in the room was subdued as people packed away their laptops and other belongings. Not only was everyone understandably very tired, but the group had got to the realisation during the afternoon that there was no quick solutions, and we would be working on the issue of the comet for some time yet.

Turning to me, the Director asked quietly, "How are you going Cyran? It's been a long day, hasn't it? I am sorry to be keeping you from other important work, but I am glad you could be part of all this."

I kept my response light and positive. "I am doing really well, thank you, but looking forward to heading home for a while."

Surprising me with being so open, Director Malone continued, "Me too, it's been a hell of a day, and I need a large glass of wine. Thank you, I will let you go. Do you have far to travel?"

"Home for me is in the UK." This was my standard answer when asked this question. "Good night, Director Malone, see you in the morning."

Out of the corner of my eye I could see Lucy standing up behind her chair and packing her laptop into her brief-case. As properly meeting Lucy had been the highlight of my day, I was keen to grab another chance to talk to her if I could. With that in mind, I walked quickly but casually around the back of the table towards where Lucy was standing.

"Hello again, Dr Lucy, before you leave I wanted to ask you a question." Lucy looked tired but she smiled, tilting her head slightly to acknowledge my hello and wait for the actual question.

"Can I organise some decent lunch for you again tomorrow?" I asked. "It was no problem doing it today, so if you have a think about what you might like, I can order it and duck out to get you food. It would make me very sad if you were faced with only terrible sandwiches again now that we are friends."

"That would be lovely thank you." Lucy's reply was simple, but just perfect. "I'll let you know some ideas in the morning."

"Good night, Dr Lucy. I hope you get some rest tonight."

Chapter 4
Lucy

By Friday morning, I was totally over being stuck in this bland grey room at NASA. Although no doubt it was cleaned every night, the room felt dirty and stale as I walked into the room first thing in the morning for our fourth straight day of taskforce meetings.

Like me, many of the taskforce members were from other cities, and long days, nights in unfamiliar beds, and time away from their families seemed to be taking a toll on everyone's moods. People had started being snappy with one another, and there was less positivity about whether we were ever going to come up with a good solution to solve the potential problem of the comet.

I was managing reasonably well, but I was tired and looking forward to the weekend when hopefully we would get to go home. This morning I had brought in a large latte with me from the cafe in the foyer of my hotel so at least I would be well caffeinated for the first half of the day.

What had really helped me stay in a good mood over the last few days was Cyran. As he had so kindly offered to do on Tuesday night, each morning Cyran asked me before we started what I would like for lunch that day. Then when lunchtime came around, he quickly disappeared to go wherever it was that he went and at the same time collected some lunch for me. I was anticipating he would do the same today. It wasn't just the food that made me happy, but also our brief snippets of conversation and his innate kindness.

Cyran's consideration for my food needs was very sweet and much appreciated, as the lunch menu did not change much and the sandwiches kept coming every day. Wednesday, Cyran had brought me a toasted sub with chicken schnitzel, spinach and melted cheese. Thursday when I had suggested pasta, he returned with an amazing spaghetti carbonara. I have a sneaking suspicion it may have come direct from Italy.

It had surprised me that no one had yet made any direct comments about the fact that Cyran was bringing me food every day and the connection that seemed to be growing between us. It seemed unlikely that no one had noticed, so perhaps everyone was just avoiding mentioning it to me.

Unfortunately, Cyran and I had not had much chance to talk, even though we were in the same room for at least ten hours each day. We had some quick interactions about food every day, but little time for talking about anything more than the meals he was so thoughtfully bringing me each day. Some more time each day to get to know him better would have been wonderful. He was very handsome, and I definitely had a thing for men with long hair. However, overall, I tended to be more attracted to someone's mind and personality than what they looked like.

Today I was hoping that we could have a chance to talk before the morning session got started. I was planning to ask Cyran for some type of Asian noodle dish for lunch if that was something he could organise. Being Friday, it was one of the days I was usually in Boston, and I often got lunch from a Vietnamese place just off campus.

After getting my laptop set up at my place on the meeting table, I stood drinking my coffee in a spot that just happened to be near the doorway to the courtyard where I knew Cyran would soon arrive. The first day he had been escorted into the room by the NASA staff like the rest of us, but since then he had been coming and going independently through the courtyard with its easy access to the sky.

Hearing the now familiar swoosh of air noise that accompanied Cyran landing at speed, I looked up and through the glass. He smiled across at me as he walked in the room and said good morning to a few people. He crossed to the table against the wall to pick up a bottle of water then came to stand beside me. Director Malone had not yet arrived to start the meeting, so it seemed we might manage a few minutes to talk.

We were both facing into the room, so at a casual glance it might look like we had both just happened to be here leaning against this piece of wall, but I knew that he had come over specifically wanting to talk to me. Just like I wanted to talk to him. There was no-one close by as everyone else was either at the coffee station or gathered around the meeting table which meant we had a little privacy.

"Hello, good morning," I said.

"Good morning, Dr Lucy. I see you have decent coffee once again. Looks like you need that today."

I agreed the coffee was much needed, and then continued, "I am getting used to the early starts, but not the bad coffee. Hopefully we won't need to be here for much longer and I can get back to my normal routines."

Turning his body in towards me slightly so he could

make eye contact, Cyran looked at me and said in a quiet voice, "So, Dr Lucy. I have really enjoyed talking to you in our very brief moments together this week. If we ever get out of this taskforce meeting, I was wondering if you would like to continue our conversation around the terrors of mustard and other scary things over a coffee in the real world?"

I sucked in a quick breath of astonishment. Expecting a question about lunch preferences, it seemed that I had instead got a date invitation. "What?" was the first thing I asked in response, surprise obviously destroying my ability to communicate properly. I followed that question up with a "Why?" followed by, "Are we allowed to do that?"

Cyran smiled. "The what is just coffee, or lunch or dinner if you would prefer, the why is because I enjoyed our conversations, however brief, and want an opportunity to get to know you better. As for being allowed, yes, I think we are two consenting adults, so that's not a problem as long as we don't talk about the taskforce work in public place."

"Yes of course, we are both adults, but, ah, how would all that work..." I waved my hand that wasn't holding my coffee around in the air, not sure how to articulate my question to address the elephant in the room, or in this case the superhero in the room.

"If I am being inappropriate, sorry, I am not sure if you have a special someone in your life, of course..."

"No. I mean no, I haven't got a special someone and I would very much like to have coffee with you." I could be clear about that issue, but I had many more questions racing through my mind. "I meant more like how would that work us going out to coffee together? I am not sure you turning up at my local cafe or us going out for dinner would be all that feasible." I slowly and deliberately looked him up and down, eyeing off his very recognisable golden eyes and alien clothing.

Cyran laughed gently, perhaps at the idea of what would happen if he did walk into a coffee shop. "Well, since we have shared our sandwich and fear of mustard secrets," he said, "I can probably tell you that sometimes when it's for an important cause like coffee with a friendly scientist, I can just wear a pair of jeans and a t-shirt and fly under the radar, so to speak. I also have contact lenses that change the colour of my eyes, so I look perfectly human."

My breath hitched again at the thought of what he would look like in regular clothes. "What sort of t-shirt?" I questioned, trying to make light of the fact that it seemed he had just shared a huge secret with me. "I don't think it would work for me if it was a heavy metal band t-shirt or one of those ones with rude toilet cartoons on them. It would have to be something cute or classy."

"How about a sporting teams shirt?" Cyran asked. "Baseball, or football? English football that is. What you would call soccer. Or something nonsporting but more intellectual, like a NASA t-shirt? I am sure there is a gift shop here in the building where I can pick one up. That might be suitable?" It seemed like he was pretending to be serious, but there was a strong hint of laughter still in his voice.

Giving the ideas a moment's thought I responded, "Something space themed would be best, seems more appropriate for you I think."

"Indeed," was his simple response.

Still not entirely sure if we were planning a date or just engaging in witty banter, I continued, "If you were wearing a t-shirt, that would be fine, we could go somewhere very casual. I live in New York, are you able to get to New York sometimes?" How silly that question sounded, as I was talking to a man who could fly and who regularly crossed the Atlantic just to get lunch.

"I can definitely get to New York anytime," Cyran's voice was still very quiet, so we couldn't be overheard, but there was clearly a hint of excitement in his words. "I am based in the UK most of the time, but I can pretty much get anywhere in the world within a few minutes if I need to, so I would be really happy to meet you somewhere in New York."

Director Malone chose that moment to walk through the main doors into the meeting room, calling out a good morning to everyone as she did. The buzz of all the conversations around the room died suddenly.

Cyran stepped back away from me and straightened his posture when heard the Director. His voice grew louder and more formal. "Right, duty calls, Dr Lucy." Gone was the relaxed and slightly flirty man I was just talking to. "I will talk to you more at lunchtime."

We were here for work, not flirting, or whatever was going on between me and Cyran, but disappointment raced through me that our brief conversation about t-shirts and coffee dates had ended so abruptly. Talking with Cyran was like relaxing in a warm bath, his words were warm and supportive and his obvious respect for me made me feel comfortable. I felt like he was interested in the real me. Unlike many of the men I interacted with socially, or unfortunately sometimes professionally, it seemed that Cyran was interested in my mind and personality, not just focused whether he could get me into bed to boost his own ego.

The idea of us having a date, coffee or dinner or whatever it would be, filled me with equal parts soft joy and strong anxiety. I liked Cyran and wanted to get to know him better, but I was not very experienced at dating as science and my career had always been my focus, and I often struggled to relate to men my own age.

My one relationship that had lasted more than a month or two was the six months I dated a fellow college student named Trevor during my second year at Tribeca University, while I was trying to have an age-appropriate second college experience. I had ended that relationship because Trevor obviously felt threatened that my grades were better than his. He started telling our friends that I was a 'real smarty pants' but he liked me anyway. Great, no thanks Trevor.

By mid-morning there seemed to be some progress in the taskforce discussions. We had come up with some reasonably workable ideas to break up and deflect the comet away from Earth, should that be required. Three satellites would go into orbit, sustained with a large battery provided by my green energy company Bright eco-electricity. They would be filled with chemical torpedoes that could be deployed to bombard and break apart the frozen gasses, dust and rock of the comet's nucleus if needed.

We were talking about battery capacity when someone's phone started ringing. Several people looked horrified at the intrusion, but expressions softened when Cyran leapt up from his chair, with an unusual looking phone in a heavy duty case in his hand. "Sorry everyone, it must be an emergency," he said, and then turned to Director Malone. "Apologies Director, I need to take this, it's the Secretary General." He put the phone up to his ear as he walked quickly out across the room and out the glass doors to the courtyard. Cyran stood for a moment outside, nodding as he listened to the caller, and then he ended the call and swiftly launched himself into the sky, departing the meeting.

The vibe in the room felt different once Cyran was

gone, at least to me if not the other taskforce participants. I was distracted and not really paying attention to the discussions, wondering instead where Cyran had gone and whether he would be able to come back.

Selfishly I was also concerned about him not being around to provide me with a lunch delivery. Unfortunately, when Director Malone announced the lunch break Cyran had not returned from his mission. I was forced to manage with a bad coffee from the coffee station in the room and a granola bar that I had in my handbag.

Throughout the course of the afternoon, the focus of the taskforce conversation gradually shifted from big picture problem solving to detailed discussions of logistics, with most of the input coming now from the NASA engineers and military personnel. We still had over four months before the comet's arrival, and there was much behind the scenes work to do, but getting to a workable solution was a major step forward.

Everyone in the room was very relieved when at about 4pm Director Malone proposed that we adjourn the taskforce discussions and reconvene in a few weeks when the finer points of logistical issues had been resolved by a subcommittee. This was quickly agreed by all taskforce members and the relief around the table was then palpable after nearly a week of very intense discussions.

Once I had packed up my laptop and other belongings and was ready to leave, I looked out towards the courtyard, pausing for a few moments in the hope that Cyran would suddenly appear. There was no need for him to come back now as the meeting was over. I was disappointed that he wasn't here so we could have a chance to say goodbye. Or perhaps a chance to not say goodbye, but rather see you soon, if he had been serious about us going out for coffee once the taskforce meeting was over.

The conference room was emptying quickly and there was no excuse for me to stay any longer. I crossed the room to say farewell to Director Malone, and then I headed out of the NASA building and down the street to my hotel. It was nice to leave the building in the daylight, see the sun shining and get what little fresh air could be found on a busy Washington DC street.

Turning my mind to logistics, I realised I could head directly from Washington to Boston tonight if I got myself organised. I would then be able to spend tomorrow catching up on my research work I had missed in the last few days before flying home to New York on Sunday. It would be quiet in my Boston lab on a Saturday and some alone time concentrating on my current project would be a great way to unwind after a gruelling week.

It was just after 9pm when I arrived at the hotel where I regularly stayed in Boston. It was a large corporate hotel right alongside the river and very close to campus. Despite being very tired, sleep still escaped me for a long time after I finally I settled into the hotel bed. My mind was busy replaying all my interactions with Cyran over the past few days in long slow loops. As I finally managed to quieten my mind and sleep caught up with me, I wondered what he was doing right now.

Chapter 5
Cyran

Not more than three minutes after I had left NASA headquarters in Washington I was standing on the top of the remaining section of a hydroelectric dam in northern India, watching millions of litres of water gush through an enormous hole in the dam wall to the valley below.

I had been told by the Secretary General when he called me that it was about an hour since the damn wall had first cracked, and the hole was rapidly expanding as the water poured through. The river at the bottom of the valley was already heavily flooded and the local authorities were very concerned about whether the rest the dam wall under my feet would remain intact. If the whole wall collapsed, that would be even more of a disaster.

My next few hours were spent plugging the hole in the dam wall with large boulders as a quick fix to stop the water flowing, and my next three days were spent helping emergency services teams rescue people from the flooding, including many who were stranded on rooftops of houses, factories and schools. By the end of the third day, I had done as much as I could. Now it was time for the army, aid workers and other government services to start tackling the massive cleanup and helping the locals rebuild.

I had gone home briefly from India to London several times. When I was out working on a natural disaster or other incident where I was needed over multiple days, I had a rule that I would take a break about every twelve hours, and fly home for some food and a super quick shower.

Now it felt good to be heading home permanently. It was the early hours of Monday morning in this time zone when I finally made it back to London. I had taken a dip in the warm waters of the Indian Ocean on the way home to rinse any lingering mud off my flight suit and then bounced through to the top of a sand dune in the Australian outback for a few minutes to dry off in the sun.

Home for me was a flat in the London suburb of Chelsea. It was on the fourth floor of a multi apartment complex originally built in the 1920s, with the larger apartments over time being subdivided into smaller spaces as London's population and housing prices grew. My parents had originally told me that I was being too extravagant when I bought the property five years ago, as it was pricey for its size.

But location was everything, particularly for me. I needed to make my home somewhere that I could easily fly in and out without being noticed. The prime selling feature of this particular flat for me had been its enclosed roof terrace providing easy private access to the sky. I had installed a code lock on the terrace door, so I did not need to carry keys, and it was a super-fast way to get in and out with having to worry about being seen by the neighbours.

Being in Chelsea it was also close to the Thames, and when coming in and out of London I could use the river as a pathway to reduce the risk of being seen and recorded by Londoners on the ground. Photos of Cyran flying across London were not much of a problem, and certainly people took photos of me all the time while I was working. What I didn't want was a photo of Cyran the superhero entering Curtis Harrington's flat ending up on social media.

Despite my parents being concerned about the money I spent on the flat, the cost was not an issue for me. I had access to a trust fund of royalty money that flowed through to me from companies with patents using technology from my home world of JandaKo. By the time I got access to the trust money at the age of 21 I could very comfortably afford to purchase a number of Chelsea flats. Instead, I bought just one, and lived off the interest from the trust, which meant that there was no need for me to juggle working a regular job to pay the bills.

Shower, food and sleep. That was my plan for the next few hours. I generally didn't need a lot of sleep, and many nights I stayed awake all night, but I had been up for about 100 hours straight by now, so I was very ready to crash. A look in the refrigerator revealed a fresh lasagna ready meal that was luckily not yet expired so I put that into the microwave before I headed into the shower. It was a family meal for four people so would just about fill me up. I was pretty sure there were no vegetables in the crisper that hadn't got slimy so I would just have to make do with the lasagna, and maybe some toast.

Once I was clean and the lasagna was hot, I sat at my scrubbed pine dining table to eat. The flat was all pale wood and white cabinetry, and it had become my safe space where I could shut out the outside world and the demands of my dual lifestyle. As I was eating, I checked my phones.

My work phone was a secure satellite phone that

worked anywhere in the world. It looked like an old-fashioned mobile phone with a small screen and keypad, and it had a heavy-duty grey case. Very few people had that phone number, and most of them were world leaders or the heads of security agencies. That phone contained a text message from the Secretary General, thanking me for my work in India and letting me know that the White House had told him that the taskforce meetings had been suspended for the immediate future. Damn. That meant no more time to spend with Lucy.

My other phone was a regular smartphone housed in the London Football Club case that my sister had bought me for Christmas last year. The missed calls log showed Mum had called me yesterday, shortly after the time I was due to be at Mum and Dad's for Sunday lunch, so I sent her a text now, telling her I was home and would be in touch soon. She wouldn't get it until the morning.

There was also a tonne of messages on my uni friends group chat, with Pete reminding everyone that the monthly pub quiz night was on Wednesday night this week, and lots of commentary about Tory's latest disaster date on Saturday night.

Between the taskforce meetings in Washington and the flooding in India it had been over a week since I had any real time to contribute to the group chat and connect with my friends. I always regretted that I must come across as an unreliable friend sometimes, seemingly randomly dropping in and out of friend group's social life and not always being available due to the demands of my work. I opened the app and put a quick message into the chat just to let everyone know I was back.

> Sorry guys, have been working, just got back into London and need about a week's sleep. Will hopefully see you Wednesday for the pub quiz.

They would all see it in the morning and know that I was still alive at least. I put my personal phone on silent and went to bed. My work phone was never on silent, as I was on call 24 hours a day seven days a week.

When I woke up four hours later, it was just after 8am. My personal phone was full of more messages from my friends, as everyone had texted and chatted while undertaking their morning routines and commutes. There were a few messages welcoming me back, some commentary on the problems on the train network and it seemed like more discussion about Tory's ongoing dating dramas.

I loved that my big university friend group was still in touch with each other. Most of us were living in London or surrounding areas. My core friend group was Tory, Pete and Josh and we spent time together very regularly, doing Wednesday night public quiz at the Pint and Plate pub about once a month, going to the occasional football match and heading to the cinema together when there was a new blockbuster action movie.

Josh was an adrenaline junkie who was always doing outdoor activities when he wasn't earning his living as a journalist at an online magazine. Tory was an economist at a large London bank and Pete was a police detective.

There was also a broader group who kept in touch via the group chat and caught up less regularly, although our friendship was still very important to us all. Dev and Emma were both teachers and had got married last year and were now talking about babies. Ange was a social worker who wrote very successful graphic novels in her spare time, and

Dylan was a hospital psychologist who spent most his time at work. Girlfriends, boyfriends and partners had flitted in and out of the group over the years for most of us but never managed to distract us from the core of our friendship.

Tory was the only one of my friends who knew my real background and identity. We had been at high school together before going to Oxford and meeting the rest of the group. As gangly thirteen year olds we had become close friends, both feeling very out of place in the world in the strange world of school. Tory had also been a new student the year I started school. For me it was my first experience with school entirely and Tory had just changed schools, moving out of a fancy private boarding school after a terrible experience with bullying.

I was dealing with having to hide everything about myself, forcing myself to move and react in ways that were not natural to me so that no-one would know I was stronger and faster than all my peers. Tory was also hiding things from everyone around him, and we bonded over being different and holding a shared fear of being exposed to the world.

These days, I maintained the fiction within my friend group that I was just Curtis Harrington, a freelance IT security consultant who needed to travel a lot for work. They all thought I was actually a spy.

After another shower to wake me up, and a cup of tea that was more a comforting ritual than anything because caffeine had no effect on my brain, I sat down and wondered what to do with the week ahead.

My mind drifted back to Lucy. I was very disappointed about having to leave the taskforce meeting on Friday without a chance to follow up on the idea of taking her out for coffee or a meal. I really liked her, she was obviously very intelligent and funny, and her smile made her face light up in a way that did weird things to my insides. All of that attracted me to her big time.

I was very inexperienced with real relationships. I had dated and had a few casual girlfriends in university, but I had never met anyone who I trusted with my alien identity or who I could see myself being in a long-term relationship with. While maintaining two different identities was hard, it was easier than the whole world knowing where I lived and who my Earth parents were, and people trying to date me for the media attention.

My phone ringing snapped me out of my deliberations. It was Tory, probably calling from his car as he drove to work. Tory lived in Kensington and worked in the City of London financial district, and he drove everywhere, paying the congestion charge and massive parking fees every day to avoid public transport.

I answered with a simple, "Hello."

"Hey Curtis, saw on the chat you were back. Just checking in quickly to see how you are doing. I assume you were in India over the weekend?"

Sighing I replied, "Yep, and it was brutal. Those poor people lost everything, and I feel like I should have stayed to do so much more."

"You know your gig is to do what you do in the emergency situation and then move on. Don't be hard on yourself." Tory was always the voice of reason. "You did an excellent job helping them, and now the long-term relief can be done by the Indian Government and UN."

"Yes, I know, but I always want to do more." Keen to change the subject I asked, "So tell me about the accountant. Were they really as bad as you claimed on the chat?"

Tory dated all genders, so I needed to be inclusive with my language.

"OMG, yes. Well, actually no, I may have exaggerated a bit for humorous effect. She seemed nice, but she talked a lot about money which as you know is a red flag for me."

"Did she know who you are?" I asked, wondering if that was the underlying cause of the date disaster.

"God no, thankfully she didn't," Tory replied. "That would have been a million times worse if she knew I wasn't just Tory who works with her flat mate, but Viscount Hector Smythe, son of the Earl of Bosthorpe. She would have had us married before the dessert course came out."

Tory sighed loudly, and then continued, "Anyway, enough about my tragic love life. I am nearly at the office. Keep safe Curtis, and I will see you Wednesday at the pub. And let's have dinner soon."

Talking to Tory about his relationship woes strengthened my resolve to try and get in touch with Lucy again. I did not want to waste the opportunity to explore whatever spark there had seemed to be between us. Whether Lucy could feel that spark with boring old Curtis as well as Cyran the superhero was a whole different question, but I hoped that I had showed her enough of my real personality that it was a possibility.

While I had not managed to get contact details for Lucy, I did know her full name and where she worked so that was a good start in tracking her down. There couldn't be too many staff members in the physics department at Endeavour University, could there?

Chapter 6
Lucy

By the Monday after the taskforce meeting had finished, I had settled back into my normal routines. My schedule over the last few days had been very light, with a quiet day on Sunday after I got home to New York. Sunday night I had caught up with my parents for dinner, which was very pleasant, except for having to keep the truth from the family about why had I been in Washington for most of the week.

Late on Tuesday morning I was in my office at the university, preparing for a guest lecture I had been asked to do for an undergraduate class the following week. There was a knock on my office door, and when I yelled "Come in" Matty the faculty administration assistant walked through my office door.

"Hey Dr Cortez, there is a visitor for you at the front desk," she said. "He said he didn't have an appointment but that his name was Curtis and I was to tell you that, quote 'He was scared of mustard and wearing a spaced themed t-shirt,' unquote. Crazy right? Shall I send him packing?"

"No!" I leapt up. My heart was pounding with a sudden

burst of nervous energy and excitement. It seemed Cyran had found me.

"Thank you Matty. I will be right out to see him." Matty turned in the doorway to leave, but I called her back, "Matty wait! Do I look alright?"

Matty laughed and took a few steps back into the room so she could take a closer look. "You look lovely," she reassured me. "So, this guy is a personal visitor then? He does seem very cute. Lucky you Dr Cortez."

"Yes, I imagine he does," I replied without knowing exactly what Cyran would look like in regular clothes.

I followed Matty out of my office, and started to rush down the corridor, but then slowed, willing myself to be calm and relaxed so I would not arrive in the reception area hot and flustered. Turning the corner from the hallway into the open area I saw a man standing leaned up against the reception desk, one elbow resting on the dark wood, smiling at me as he heard my approach.

It was Cyran, but not quite. Gone was the striking flight suit that made him one of the most identifiable people on the planet. Gone, hidden in a messy bun on the back of his head was his signature long flowing hair. His striking copper eyes were now a regular shade of blue. But his smile was the same, still the warm gentle smile I had seen in our secret conversations during the taskforce meetings at NASA.

Instead of his flight suit, Cyran wore tight fitting jeans, the promised t-shirt, and a grey leather coat, cut in the style of a long line trench coat. The t-shirt itself was a pale green one themed with the logo of a major space movie franchise. He had a pair of aviator sunglasses perched on top of his head and carried a black leather backpack over one shoulder.

As I walked forward into the room, he stopped leaning against the reception desk and stood up straighter.

"Hello Dr Lucy, it's lovely to see you again." As he spoke his smile widened and a playful tone crept into his voice. "I was, well, I was in the neighbourhood and wondering if you were free for lunch today?"

My mind flopped about trying to make sense of what he just said. In the neighbourhood? But he can fly!

I took a deep breath to calm my rapidly beating heart and my slightly overwhelmed brain. "Hello, *Curtis*," I said, placing perhaps a little more vocal emphasis on his name than would be normal as I tried it out. "It is lovely to see you again too."

Conscious that we had an audience as Matty was sitting nearby behind the reception desk, I invited Cyran back to my office for some privacy. "Would you like to come down to my office?" I asked, gesturing down the hallway.

We walked quietly side by side until we reached my office door, which was still open from when I had burst through a few moments ago. "This is me," I said and ushered him through with a wave of my hand.

"It's a nice office," Cyran commented as he walked in and looked around the room. "Much bigger than what I remember of the professors' offices at Oxford."

Holding back the million questions that comment raised, I closed the door to give us privacy and started the conversation by stating the obvious. "You are here, in my office, in New York, wearing a t-shirt. And your hair is up, and you have cool sunglasses."

"Yes. To all of the above." Cyran smiled, leaned forward and lowered his voice a little. "Just to clear though, you do recognise me from Washington, right? I, um, well, I am dressed a bit different from what you probably remember, and I have my contact lenses in today so I can blend in."

That gave me an excuse to stare at him a little more closely, my eyes slowly moving up and down his body. His normal people clothes clung well to his body, his hair was more casual up and off his face, and he slouched a little, with a more relaxed posture than I remembered from the time we spent together in Washington.

Cyran laughed. "Do I pass inspection?"

"I'm sorry, and yes, very much so. I mean yes, you do pass inspection, but sorry I should not have been doing such blatant inspecting. And of course I recognise you. You look the same but different, except for your eyes, of course."

"No, it's okay," he said, suddenly losing the laugh and sounding more serious. "I was actually very nervous you wouldn't like this version of me. There are not many people who know both this me," he paused and pointed at himself, waving his hand up and down his body, "and who also know the other me," he said swooshing his hand through the air in a plane taking off gesture.

"So far both seem pretty good to me, and I am very pleased to see you again. How did you know where to find me?"

"When you introduced yourself that first day of the taskforce you said you worked here at the university. I just asked everyone on campus where to find the sexy scientist lady and they all pointed in this direction," he joked. "Seriously though, once I got up the courage to come and find you, all it took was a bit of online searching and a look at the campus map and here I am."

"Okay wow." Continuing with the questions I asked, "So, you're Curtis when you're dressed like this? Is that your real name?"

"Yes, Curtis is the name my adoptive parents gave me when I went to live with them. They wanted me to have a nice regular English name so I could blend in and live a relatively normal life without always having to be recognisable as the world-famous alien orphan. Curtis was my mum's grandfather's name, so they used that."

"Both are my real names," he continued. "I just use whichever suits what I am doing. The world knows Cyran by the flight suit and the superhero stuff, but when dressed like this and having a pint at the pub with friends or asking sexy professors out to lunch I need to be Curtis. If we went to lunch while I was wearing my flight suit, we would be mobbed, and your picture would be on every social media platform within about five minutes."

My thoughts paused on two things Cyran had just said. Going viral for being out in public with a superhero was a very sobering idea and something I wanted to avoid at all costs. The second, much more pleasant, thought was that Cyran had admitted that he was attracted to me, having just described me as sexy twice in this conversation. That idea made me feel tingly all over.

"Okay then Curtis it is," I said, focussing back in on the conversation. "And yes, I would very much like to have lunch with you, today. I am free until 2 o'clock so we have plenty of time."

I tried to lighten my tone a little. "Did your searching give you some ideas of where to eat? We need to go off campus if we want to avoid the hordes of hungry students. There's a great Thai place just a block away if you like Thai food. But I'm happy to go anywhere you like."

Cyran lightly clapped his hands together. "That sounds perfect, I love going to Asian food places as I can get away with ordering lots of dishes without anyone thinking it's too strange. I am very hungry, particularly as it is basically dinner time for me. I am on London time."

With that settled, I grabbed my bag, and we headed out into the world. I did not need a coat. It was early May, and spring was here, so the weather was perfect for walking the streets of this always busy city. The sun was shining and there was only a hint of breeze.

As we approached the restaurant, Cyran gently placed a hand on my shoulder and asked me to wait a second. "Before we go in, I have a favour to ask. When we are out in public like this I need to be, and you will need to be, sorry, well a bit discreet about my job and my background." He paused, shaking his head slightly. "What I mean is I cannot talk about some stuff for fear of being overheard and revealing my identity to the world."

"So no asking the 'so what's it like being an alien' question in the restaurant, is that what you mean?' I asked quietly.

"Pretty much, yes. If that's okay."

Wanting to reassure him that I was not interested in getting to know him just because he could fly, I said gently, "I am keen to get to know you, both sides of you. Not just a fly boy fan girl this one." I said pointing at myself. "I also really like men in leather jackets, so the moment you turned up rocking that look, you were pretty much guaranteed at least one date."

"Excellent to know. More leather jackets. Thank you for all that and come on let's get the food now." Cyran seemed slightly embarrassed by my words and let go of my shoulder.

The restaurant had seating on the sidewalk under a bright green awning, a series of interconnecting room spaces inside and an inviting outdoor garden at the side in a converted alleyway. I had been here several times before for lunches with colleagues, or working dinners with my research team, and both the atmosphere and the food had always been good.

"Inside or outside?" I asked Cyran as we walked through the front door. "The garden is really pretty if you don't mind a bit of sunshine."

"Outside sounds great if you are comfortable with that."

Our server was approaching, and I asked for an outside table. There was not much of a crowd, and we easily got a table for two under one of the shade umbrellas in the garden. And so began our first official date.

Opening the menu, Cyran asked me whether I had any recommendations for food. "Everything I had here before has been good. There are no sandwiches on the menu, and I don't think anything with mustard so it's all safe," I joked, recalling our very first conversation about food in the courtyard at NASA.

"Good to know." He laughed his warm rich laugh that sent little bursts of sparkly joy racing up and down my insides. At that moment I felt like I just wanted to sit here in the garden and listen to him laugh for the rest of my life.

Cyran continued to talk about food. "Do you want to share a bunch of dishes then? I am pretty hungry, and so if we order a few things, I am sure I will eat them."

"Sounds good, I can never choose between the Pad Thai, which is fabulous here by the way, and a green chicken curry. That way I can have a bit of both."

The next hour was perfect in every way. We had a huge range of food, after Cyran ordered not only my two favourite dishes, but also a fried rice and a garlic beef. We chatted and laughed together as we ate.

Cyran was warm and witty, his intelligence and broad-minded interest in the world coming through as we talked about current events, and shared information about ourselves.

At first my mind tried to race ahead to all the 'what ifs' of me having a potential relationship with this wonderful man. Did we like each other enough to overcome the fact that we lived on different continents, both had very busy jobs, family lives and big secrets?

But then I relaxed and allowed myself to be drawn back into the moment, to just enjoy Cyran's company in the here and now. There would be time later, when we were at least finished our first date, and hopefully moving on to a second, to worry about logistics for a relationship that didn't yet exist.

Cyran told me he loved K-pop music, hated spinach and could not understand the US political system. He told he had just one sibling, an older sister, who was a school-teacher and a busy solo mom to two amazing kids, and that his adopted parents had recently retired to the same small village outside London where she lived, to help out and spend lots of time with the grandkids.

"My Dad worked for the UK Government as a linguist for many years," he explained quietly, "and he and Mum were on the foster parent list as they wanted more children after Beth, my sister, was adopted. That's how they ended up with me when it was decided that I should live with a 'normal' family. Basically, because Dad had the relevant security clearance."

Cyran continued, "It worked out really well for me, as I needed stability and normality, particularly as I was still grieving the loss of my first family."

That comment made me sad for Cyran, but I didn't want to ask too many questions. That seemed too personal a topic for a first date, and not something to discuss in a public setting.

So instead, I shared that I had four siblings, three older and one younger, and that my family was big, warm, often too loud and very much in each other's lives.

"We lived in New York, in Queens, until I got my first scholarship to the Logan Institute in Boston," I explained. "And then Mom and Dad packed the up whole family, except for my oldest brother, who was already in the Army by that point and moved to Boston so that they could support me while I was at college."

"Wow, that's intense, how did you feel about that?"

Curtis's question about my college days had been casual and his tone friendly, but it triggered a wave of anxiety about sharing my secrets. But I didn't want to break the spell of the trust growing between us that afternoon, so I told him the truth.

"Well, I was only twelve at the time and way too young to leave home, so I felt it was a really good idea."

Chapter 7
Cyran

Twelve? Did Lucy just say she started college at age twelve?

"That's amazing." So many questions were swirling around in my brain, dying to be asked, but I didn't want to offend her by asking the wrong thing. "I am trying not to pry if you don't want to share, but wow, twelve seems really young."

"Yeh, it was." Lucy spoke softly, and those few words were full of emotion. "I graduated high school at the end of what should have been sixth grade, after spending a few years at an advanced curriculum school. I then did my undergraduate degree in physics at Logan Technology Institute in Massachusetts, and then my first PhD. They have a young students support program, so I got well looked after, but it was very weird being so much younger than my classmates."

I nodded and smiled across at Lucy, quietly signalling that I was listening and keen for her to continue.

"When I was 18, we all came back to New York. My

parents were keen to move back home to Queens, and I wanted to have a real college experience with some people my own age. I moved into the dorms at Tribeca University and started another undergraduate degree. That one was in business management which was very different from all the science I had previously done. I did keep going with science as well, doing a second PhD in engineering at Endeavour, so I was studying at two New York universities at the same time. It was busy but worth it."

"At the moment I am on staff at both Logan Technology Institute and Endeavour, so I do a fair bit of commuting between here and Boston," Lucy continued, a hint of shyness coming through it her voice. "It's mostly research and supervising graduate students though, I don't have an active teaching load at either university. So that makes it a bit easier."

Despite how impressive this all sounded, Lucy seemed to feel shy about admitting her achievements. Perhaps she had been somehow judged or ridiculed by others in the past? Or did she not think it was attractive to be so smart? If that was true, it was certainly not how I felt about it, about her. Smart was definitely sexy in my book.

Realising I was taking a bit too long thinking through my response to her explanation, I jumped back into the conversation. "That is amazing, you are amazing, awesome," I babbled. Really? What was coming out of my mouth now?

Getting my thoughts together I continued, "In all seriousness, you must work really hard being a professor at two high profile colleges and juggling different work demands. I personally find smart people very sexy."

Lucy blushed hard and ducked her head to look at the table. "Thank you. That's sweet of you."

The restaurant around us had been gradually emptying, as people finished their lunches and headed back into the real world. The garden felt quiet and private as Lucy and I were one of only two groups left.

Unfortunately, our lunch would also have to end soon as Lucy was due back at work by 2 o'clock. Talking with Lucy was easy and relaxed. She appeared to be dealing with the whole me being an alien thing very well. The fact that she was comfortable with being discreet about my identity was also a major plus.

Taking the initiative, I told Lucy, "I have really enjoyed myself today, I like talking to you, spending time with you. Would you be willing to go somewhere with me again sometime soon?"

Lucy's face broke into a smile. "I enjoyed myself too, thank you. It was a bit surreal, you turning up like that unexpectedly, but our lunch has been extremely nice."

"But just to be very clear," Lucy continued as my heart plummeted. "Are you asking me for a date or just another casual something? I would like it to be a date, but I don't want there to be any ambiguity." She paused and chewed her lip self-consciously. "Sorry. I am often told I am a bit too direct."

I sighed with relief. Direct was good for me, I functioned best in social situations where everyone said what they meant, rather than relying on nuance and innuendo.

"Definitely a date." Reaching across the table, my left hand went to rest lightly on top of her right hand, which was sitting on the table. I looked up at her face, and noticed her brown eyes were sparkling. "I would like to get to know you better, to spend lots more time with you."

Locking eyes across the table, we just sat there and

smiled at each other for a few seconds. I felt like we had made a strong connection and that there was the potential of something possibly great starting between us. Lucy broke eye contact with me, withdrawing her hand from under mine and reached down into her handbag that was sitting under the table.

"Right, logistics," she said suddenly, opening her phone that was now in her hand, presumably to look at her calendar. "We need to do some planning about when and where, etc. I don't suppose you know what your work schedule is going to be like on the weekend? And can you tell me about date parameters?"

I leaned back in my chair and laughed. Date parameters, that was an abrupt change of approach. "I haven't had that many dates in recent years," I admitted sheepishly. "But I suppose I do have some parameters."

Most of my romantic interactions over the last few years had been with women who my friends had tried to set me up with, including one terrible blind date with a schoolteacher who was absolutely lovely, but who I had to abandon before dessert to stop a bridge collapsing in New Zealand.

"I just want to know what suits and what does not suit for you, given your job constraints, the time zone issues, and your need to avoid mustard at all costs." I could sense Lucy was trying to soften her approach.

After thinking about it for a moment, I outlined to Lucy that we would need to go somewhere where I could discreetly leave suddenly if I needed to, so nothing that involved travelling, like a boat trip, or a room where I could not leave without drawing major attention.

Time zones were not an issue, I could be anywhere

anytime, and my sleep was flexible as well as I didn't need much rest. My regular commitments were occasional evenings with my friends, and Sunday lunch or Sunday dinner with my parents. Other than that, I was free most days, depending on what was happening in the world in terms of freak weather, other natural disasters or emergencies.

"Somewhere with food options would be good, as I am always hungry, but I can work around mustard issues as I will be wearing civilian clothes. And finally, a place where there are things you can do without me would be ideal, so that should I did need to pop out, you will not be left sitting around feeling uncomfortable."

Lucy looked at me intently as I finished explaining all this. "So there actually are parameters," she noted. "Quite a few in fact."

"Sorry, yes." My anxiety spiked over whether she was saying this was all too hard.

"That's okay though, I am still very keen for another date," Lucy clarified.

"If you have not been put off by all the parameters, how about we do something this weekend?" I asked, hoping she wasn't one of these people who was constantly busy and booked social things weeks ahead. I did not want to wait weeks to see her again.

"I am free on Saturday during the day," Lucy told me. "I've got a family thing late on Saturday afternoon for my niece's birthday, but I am free until midafternoon. Are you okay with a lunchtime date?"

I said that I was, and Lucy continued, "If you are happy to come to New York, we can go exploring or perhaps go to the Zoo. Have you ever been to the Central Park Zoo?"

I had flown over the top of the Zoo many times and so was familiar with what it looked like from the sky but had never seen it at ground level. "No, I haven't been there yet."

As that seemed to meet all the date parameters, we agreed to meet at 10am at the main entrance to the Central Park Zoo. I did offer to pick Lucy up at her apartment, but she brushed me off. I wondered briefly if she was embarrassed by her apartment in some way.

Lucy looked at her watch and jumped up. "Okay, I really need to go now. I will see you on Saturday. I will pay for lunch on the way out. My treat. No argument," she said pretty much all in one breath.

"Okay, thanks," was the only thing I could think of to say in the moment, but I wanted to protest that she didn't need to pay for my lunch, particularly as I was the one who had ordered so much food.

She turned towards the door to leave but then turned back towards me. Leaning down to whisper in my ear she asked, "Should we swap numbers? Is it alright for me to have your phone number or is that a national security secret?"

"No, that's fine. My phone number is not any sort of secret if you save it in your contacts under Curtis." I grabbed my personal phone from my jacket pocket, and we quickly swapped details. One of my two phone numbers was in fact a security secret, but Lucy didn't need to know that right now.

Lucy bent forward and kissed me lightly on the check, then turned away. She walked across the restaurant garden and through the door to the main part of the restaurant and was gone. I knew logically that she had to go back to work, and that I had interrupted her day, but I felt bereft that our lunch was now over. Today was only Tuesday, and our next date on Saturday seemed so much too far away.

Sitting in a nearly empty restaurant was not helping, so I gathered up my coat, thanked the wait staff and wandered out into the busy streets of New York. I walked a block away from the restaurant and then I ducked into an alley, changed my clothes and took to the sky.

Chapter 8
Lucy

The rest of Tuesday went by in an exceedingly normal way, despite me having a background feeling that something major had just changed in my life.

I sat through my afternoon of discussions with my graduate students and then an online meeting with some colleagues in San Francisco about a possible joint research project, all while part of my brain power was off trying to process what had just happened with Cyran. Or should I be calling him Curtis now?

I was flattered that Cyran had gone to the effort to track me down in the real world after our time together in Washington. He must have felt the connection we had made in that dingy NASA conference room, just like I did.

It was early evening before my day finished, and I had jumped in a cab to get home, too tired to contemplate walking. Home for me was an original early 1900s brownstone on W95th Street on the Upper West Side. It was two blocks from Central Park, and walking distance to the university on a nice day.

The house had been a family home for its entire history. I had the occasional twinge of guilt at living alone in a large house in a very crowded city, but this house was my sanctuary. I had everything I needed here, including a gym in the basement for exercise, a home theatre, and a small very private terrace for some outdoor space. There were three bedrooms, a large study for my work, and a gourmet kitchen that I rarely used. One of the many reasons I had fallen in love with this brownstone when I was house hunting was the deep soaking bathtub with spa jets in the master suite. It had quickly become my favourite place to de-compress after an intense day.

I had told Cyran much of my back story this afternoon at lunch but had left out an important fact about myself and my history. As I had revealed to Cyran, I had started college at twelve, heading to Boston on a full scholarship after finishing high school in an accelerated program for high IQ kids here in New York. My parents, particularly my father, had encouraged me in my love of math and science since a very early age, and before I even formally started school, I was reading my older siblings' textbooks and peppering my father with science questions.

When I was fifteen and just starting my PhD program in physics, I had made a major scientific breakthrough, inventing a subatomic green energy generation system. This revolutionary new power source, which I named eco-electricity, means that a battery the size of a laptop can power an electric car for 10 years without needing to be recharged, or a battery the size of a car can power a whole suburb for a year.

My invention had eventually made me rich, but not famous. As I had only been a child, and a young woman of colour, my parents, with the support of the university, had decided that they would not give the public my name when announcing a major environmentally friendly scientific discovery amid ongoing climate change political wars. In all public materials, they referred to me just as Professor Smith. I had never regretted this decision, particularly given the crazy nature of some of the conspiracy theories and online hate that had swirled for many years about the new technology which was slowly changing the way we powered the world.

When I turned eighteen, I set up a company called Bright Eco-electricity to distribute this new green energy technology across the world. One of the early adopter industries had been the tech world, which was hungry for energy to power the massive servers need to support artificial intelligence and quantum computing. Shortly afterwards I sold a major stake in Bright to a global electronics and energy firm which could mass produce and market my invention, and I became a billionaire overnight. With my initial payout and ongoing profit shares, now at 28 years old I was one of the richest women in the United States.

Part of the sale deal was that I stayed involved with the company, and these days I still had a seat on the board of Bright Eco-electricity. I also spent a few hours each week working at the New York offices focusing on philanthropic programs to help developing countries introduce clean energy. Most people I worked with there did not know I was the inventor of the product we were sharing with the world.

After a long soak in my bath, I headed downstairs to my kitchen and heated up some empanadas that my mother had sent home with me after family dinner on Sunday night. Providing food was Mom's love language and as I did not really cook at all, she was constantly providing me with meals for the fridge and freezer.

Mom regularly made the trip into Manhattan from where she and Dad lived in the Astoria neighbourhood in Queens, usually on a Friday when I was in Boston, with a cooler bag perched on the seat beside her full of food. Living in the heart of New York it was not like I was limited in easy access to restaurants and online delivery, but I really appreciated the love behind the food.

I had grown up Astoria, amongst a close-knit group of mostly immigrant families. My Dad had worked in maintenance at La Guardia airport, and Mom was a teacher's aide working with special needs children. Back then we had a three-bedroom apartment for the six of us.

Mom and Dad had returned to the same neighbourhood when we moved back from Boston when I was eighteen, keen to reconnect with old friends and neighbours. These days they lived in a renovated freestanding house that I had bought for them when I sold my company. It was nestled in a quiet suburban street, close to the train and nearby all their friends. They had retired early when we returned to New York, my money giving them financial security. Nowadays they kept busy volunteering in the community and helping my sister and brothers raise the grandkids.

Needing help to process everything that had happened that day with Cyran, I texted my best friend Kane to see if he was available for a chat. Kane worked long hours, in a role that he was very passionate about, just like I did, and I didn't want to disturb him even this late.

Kane called me about two minutes later. "Hello gorgeous, I am just getting home, so definitely free for a chat. What's happening in your world that can't wait until I see you tomorrow?"

"Well, it's a bit of a long story," I replied, "But I sort of had a date today, and I wanted to tell you all about it."

"Oooooh!!! With an actual live man? All the details please."

Obviously, I couldn't share *all* the details of my date with Cyran with Kane, to maintain Cyran's privacy, but our story still made sense with a few key details changed.

"Well, you know how I was in Washington for that conference last week? I met him there and we talked quite a bit at the lunch breaks. I thought he was witty and charming, but then he had to leave suddenly for a work emergency, and I thought that was it, I would not see him again. But then this morning he turned up at my office, having tracked me down, because he wanted to take me out to lunch. And so, we went to lunch and had a wonderful time and now I like him a whole lot more."

"Wow. Does this fabulous man have a name?"

"Oh, sorry, yes, his name is Curtis, and he is English."

"Oooh, English, excellent." I could hear Kane clapping his hands down the phone line. I knew he would have me on speaker or have his headphones in as he loved to talk with his hands even when he was on the phone. "I am getting strong Mr Darcy vibes here. Is he tall, dark and looks good in a wet white shirt?"

I laughed both at the visual and Kane's enthusiasm. "Yes, he is tall, no not dark but more dark blonde, and I don't yet know about the whole shirt thing. The first time I met him he was wearing his work clothes and today he was wearing jeans and an amazing long leather jacket over a t-shirt."

"And how are you feeling about all this Lucy?" I could

hear the caring behind Kane's question. "You don't date much, but you obviously said yes to this hottie?"

"Yes, I really like him. I felt respected when he first talked to me, and like he was not threatened by my intelligence. He calls me Dr Lucy, trying to be playful I think, but it is really sweet. We are going out again on Saturday to the Central Park Zoo on another casual date. I am both excited about it and very nervous. What if he decides he doesn't like me?"

"Don't panic Lucia." Kane was using my full name, so I knew this was serious. "A, of course that he is going to keep liking you, you are fabulous, and B, well that is what dates are for, to get to know people. You need to go see some cute animals together and see where it all goes."

I heard a chime in the background of the phone call, which I recognised as the doorbell for Kane's apartment. Like me, Kane rarely cooked during the week, so it was probably a food delivery. Unlike me though, Kane could actually cook when he decided he wanted to and had the time.

"Is that your dinner arriving?" I asked him. "I will let you go so you can eat. We can chat tomorrow at work."

"Okay sweetie, thanks. But ring me later if you are having a meltdown or need me, promise?"

"Goodnight Kane, I will be fine thanks. Enjoy your dinner."

Kane and I had been best friends for almost 10 years, and he was one of the key people in my life. Kane was someone who I could trust enough to be the real me around, rather than having to be on show the whole time, and I knew that feeling was mutual. We first met in college when we were both nineteen and had shared an apartment for the last year of our studies, after we both moved out of the dorms.

We had shared several classes as freshmen but only really got to know each other the next year when we did a group project together for a class on the social impact role of corporations. Each group in the class was doing the same project, and our assignment was to design a philanthropic program to establish a self-sustaining community support program to help low wage and unwaged Americans meet their daily essential needs. Our theoretical corporations would put up seed funding of $50 million.

Most of the groups focused how to fund varying organisations and charities to give direct support. Our group's model was different, and it was Kane's idea to establish a business with the seed money and use the profits to support ongoing community outreach programs.

This theoretical business was to be a community supermarket, placed in a low-income neighbourhood, where the focus was on selling low-cost fresh food and where basic essentials like toothbrushes, soap and personal care items were available for free. Our proposal involved the supermarket having a medical care clinic attached, showers and toilets available to all, not just customers, and a 24-hour cafeteria area which was a safe and inclusive space, where free hot drinks and pizza were provided for anyone who needed a meal. Our supermarket also helped the community by paying its staff a real living wage, providing health insurance benefits to all employees, and having an onsite childcare centre.

We called our pretend business Kane's Community Mart. Our other group member Ellie had a brother studying graphic design, and she got him to design us a logo for the supermarket.

At the end of the semester the three of us had to pitch our proposal to a meeting of the 'board of directors' of the fake corporation, who were college staff roped in for the presentations. On the day of the pitch, we all wore t-shirts I had got printed with the Kane's Community Mart logo on them, and we brought baskets of real fruit and vegetables into the lecture hall to help give more of an impression that we were standing in a real supermarket. The board of directors had liked our pitch, and we had got a great mark for the project.

Two years later, on the day that we both graduated from college, I suggested to Kane that he should establish a real Kane's Community Mart, offering to provide him with the $50 million or however much was needed in seed money to get it all started.

Once Kane had recovered from the shock of discovering his best friend was a billionaire, he had set to work, guided by an experienced CEO, and turned our college project into reality. These days Kane is the company's CEO and Ellie and I are both on the board of directors. The logo designed by Ellie's brother is now being used on signage for the chain of more than fifty Kane's Community Mart stores across the country. I was very proud of what the three of us had achieved.

Chapter 9
Cyran

I got home to London just a few minutes after I left the restaurant in New York. With the time difference, it was now just before 6pm and the streets were full of commuters leaving work and heading home, scurrying along with heads down and umbrellas up battling against a persistent drizzle. I was drenched from hitting a storm in the mid-Atlantic and headed straight to a hot shower.

Normally I did not have to worry much about how to spend my time. Between my superhero job and spending time with family and my friends I was kept busy. I also did yoga, taking classes in several different countries, and sometimes volunteered with a local community group supporting unhoused people.

I usually didn't mind my own company, but tonight a quiet night in did not appeal at all. Now that I had my date on Saturday with Lucy to really look forward to, the week ahead seemed long and empty. In need of company, I reached out to my friend Tory to see if he had plans after work or was up for a meal. Thankfully he was free, and an hour later I was sitting in a gastro pub in Canary Wharf waiting for him to arrive. I had taken the Tube rather than making my own way across the city. Public transport was much slower than flying, but often more convenient in that I didn't need to find somewhere to change when I got where I was going.

The drizzle from earlier had turned into steady downpour and the streets were now very grey with heavy rain. Tory rushed in out of the rain, shaking his umbrella and placing it in the tub set up by the door for that purpose. He looked like a quintessential young English businessman dressed in a tailored suit and long wool coat. His thick dark hair, which would have been carefully gelled into place this morning, was now slightly unruly, having got damp in the journey from the office.

Tory had studied economics and international finance at university and then joined the graduate program of a prestigious investment bank. He rapidly risen through several promotions, earning his place as a senior economist through a combination of intellect and working an insane number of hours each week.

"Hello Curtis. Lovely night for it."

I stood up to shake hands. "Hi, thanks for meeting with me on such a crap night. I am glad you were free."

Tory shrugged off his coat and draped it around the back of his chair. "Let's order straight away as I am hungry, and I am sure you are too. Then let's settle in and you can tell me all your news."

The pub had online ordering at the table, which was a top contender for the best invention of the last ten years in my opinion, so we didn't have to fight our way to the bar. A few minutes later I had organised a burger and a beer for each of us.

"So," Tory asked when I had stashed my phone away.

"What brings us out on this damp evening? Not that I ever mind a catchup, but are you okay?"

"Yes, short version is I'm very okay. Longer version is that I do have some news, good news I think." I paused as the beers arrived at the table, and I thanked our waitperson before continuing.

"I met a girl, well a woman, and I think that this has real potential. I like her a lot." I paused again, waiting for Tory's reaction.

"Well that's honestly unexpected." Tory shook his head slightly and then continued. "Sorry, that sounded wrong. Fabulous news, just great, tell me more. Particularly, which one of you met this woman, and does she have a name or is that a secret?"

I laughed and leaned forward slightly. With the noise around us there was little chance of anyone overhearing, but I thought about how best to phrase this in a way that did not sound ridiculous without giving away any of my secrets in a crowded restaurant.

"Well, her name is Lucy, and she is an American. The first time we met she met the other me when I was working in the US, but the second time she met this one." I waved my hands up and down in front of my myself, trying to indicate my normally dressed self. "When I took her out to lunch today."

"You told her already?" That Tory was shocked was obvious from both his tone of voice and the look on his face.

"Well yes, I needed to if I was going to be able to see her in the real world," I replied. "We were together for a few days at this thing I can't talk about, and I really really liked her, she is cute and funny, and we had a connection. I asked her out, telling her that I sometimes wore normal clothes and could pass for a regular guy."

"I had to leave for the India thing before I got her phone number, so I tracked her down at her office then took her out to lunch today. She was surprised but seemed very happy to see me. We have another date on the weekend."

"I am really glad for you, but just a bit surprised by how quickly all that happened," Tory said. "Particularly because you have been so keen on not telling your other friends your secret. Is this Lucy trustworthy do you do think? Have you run a background check on her?" Tory did have a valid point about my keeping secrets from my friends.

"It's all good, Lucy's definitely trustworthy. Sorry I can't tell you where or why I met her, but I know that the people who run the place where we met would have done all of that."

"Oh, she's in the secret squirrel government club." This was more of a statement from Tory than a question, possibly because he knew I wouldn't answer a direct question.

I ignored Tory's statement and tried to change the focus of the conversation away from things directly related to national security. "Anyway, Lucy's a scientist, a physics professor and researcher."

When our food arrived the conversation quickly turned to other topics, including England's chances in the upcoming football World Cup. Any conversation was comfortable with Tory. He was one of the very few people in the world in whose company I could just be me and not have to pretend or think too hard about what I was saying or force my body to act 100 percent human. We sat in the pub and chatted far later than we should have given Tory had work the next day, relaxing in the quiet joy of our great friendship.

The weather was no better the following night when I travelled across London to meet my friends for our regular Wednesday night pub quiz catchup. The rain was coming in sideways in a determined effort to get everyone as wet as possible and all but the sturdiest umbrellas were being blown inside out by the wind. I ran out of the Tube station and headed up the road to the Plate and Pint pub with my head down and my hand up on my head holding the hood of my jacket in place to keep the rain off my face.

My backpack was slung over my left shoulder. It looked just like a daypack for hiking or a large school bag. This was my work bag containing my flight suit and boots and I took it everywhere with me so I could dash off if there was an emergency. After considerable practice, I could get my suit and boots on, take my contact lenses out, and put my civilian clothes back in the bag in just under thirty seconds.

The Plate and Pint pub had been operating on the corner here since the 1880s and had seen much of London change around it. Today there was still dark wood on the walls, small tables and a long bar running the length of the back wall. Pushing the heavy front door open, I relaxed as the Pint's familiar and comforting warmth and mixture of sounds and smells wrapped around me. The pub was like a second home to me, as my friends had been gathering here regularly since just after we all graduated from uni and moved to, or back to, London. We had started going to pub trivia quiz nights in Oxford when we all at university and kept the tradition on in London as a way of keeping in touch.

I looked towards the side wall where we usually got our table. It was reasonably quiet as it was still early and most of the crowd of teams for the quiz night had not yet arrived.

Pete was seated at our regular table, obviously having come direct from work. He was wearing business clothes but now with his tie off and folded neatly on the table.

"Hi, good to see you." Pete welcomed me over and then added, "Josh and Tory are at the bar if you want to add your order in."

"Hey Curtis." That voice came from off to the side, and I turned towards Tory who was yelling from across the room where he and Josh were leaning against the bar. "What do you want - a beer?"

I walked about halfway towards the bar, so I could provide my answer without hollering across the room like Tory had done. "Yes, please. Whatever you're drinking." I was not fussy, particularly as the alcohol did not have any effect on me.

Heading back to the table, I sat next to Pete while we waited for the others to get our drinks. We chatted about the weather first, in accordance with social norms, and then switched to analysing the recent international cricket test match, which I had missed while overseas, but had caught up on scores and highlights earlier today to prepare for just this conversation.

Tory and Josh came back with the beers, each of them juggling two pints and two packs of crisps. The snacks were to keep us going until we got around to ordering food according to Tory. I was very grateful as always that he was constantly finding sneaky ways to feed me more calories. I was pretty sure he would eat just a couple and then push his bag over towards me to finish off.

Josh leaned forward across the table. "So Curtis, we haven't seen or heard much from you for a couple of weeks. Where did you and your trusty backpack go on adventure this time?" Josh had never been shy about asking nosy questions, which was part of what make him a great journalist. He also never passed up an opportunity to tease me about the fact that I took my backpack everywhere.

"Glasgow," I replied quickly, randomly picking somewhere that sounded unexciting. "To help a large organisation with an impending hardware and incoming content interface impact problem."

"Right, that sounds thrilling, if that was what you were actually doing." Josh laughed like he didn't believe me, which was fair enough really given I had not actually been in Glasgow. While his teasing was always good natured it was regular, and I always felt guilty about keeping secrets from my best friends.

When we were all at university together, I had been actively trying to hide my alien identity. My parents, while very loving, were keen for me to have a normal life and to them that meant ignoring the fact that I had been born on another planet and suppressing my alien abilities and characteristics. That had made me uncomfortable about being who I actually was, let alone talking to anyone about it. As the years had passed, I had started to worry that if I suddenly confessed now my friends would be hurt and judge me for keeping the secret from them for so long. I could not win with that one.

That Wednesday night I kept the existence of Lucy a secret as well. While I had told Tory, I wasn't yet ready to tell the rest of my friends about something that was so new. She and I needed to get through at least a few more dates first, particularly as it was going to be difficult to explain the whole Lucy lives in the US angle to everyone when I did tell them.

Coffee with a Superhero

I might not have been talking about Lucy, but I was certainly thinking about her. I was looking forward to our date on Saturday immensely and really hoping that nothing would disrupt our time together.

Chapter 10
Lucy

On Saturday I woke early. I was both excited and nervous at the same time about my date with Cyran. I had thought about him constantly in the few days since he had turned up unexpectedly at my office and whisked me off for lunch, reliving our conversations many times and trying not to second guess whether anything I had said had been silly.

My work week had been busy and that had helped keep me focused. As usual I had spent Wednesday morning at the Kane's Community Mart headquarters, catching up with the important work that Kane and his team were doing. As a non-executive director, I didn't have a specific day-to-day role, but I liked to stay involved.

That was followed by a Bright Eco-electricity board meeting on Wednesday afternoon, at which we discussed the company providing a massive battery to supply operational power for the satellites the NASA taskforce was building, and then I caught a late flight to Boston so I could start early in the lab the following morning.

Thursday and Friday were my standard days to be in

Boston, and I loved getting engrossed in the work my team was doing on how eco-electricity could be used to power various technologies including long range space flight. This week had been a bit different because a significant chunk of my day on Friday was taken up not by my regular lab work but rather a secure teleconference with several NASA engineers about Project Haggerston, the code name they were using for building the satellites to combat the comet.

Now it was Saturday, and I was not feeling well rested. Today was going to be a long day, with my date with Cyran being followed by my niece's birthday party and then family dinner at my parents' house. The birthday party was at an indoor play place in Queens, and I was going along to help my sister and brother-in-law wrangle the group of excited six-year-olds.

Over breakfast, I read through the Plan Your Visit Page on the Central Park Zoo website. I liked having information in advance about anything I was doing to reduce any chance of anxiety, and particularly today it was important I was well prepared as I wanted everything to go smoothly. The weather was looking good, with no rain forecast, so that was a good start to my day with Cyran.

Clothing wise, I settled on something very simple. Jeans, a t-shirt and floral scarf, pink sneakers, and a light-weight black sweater. I wasn't going to wear uncomfortable clothes to try and impress someone. I put on sunscreen and grabbed a hat.

By 9.30am I was ready, and I left the house and walked out to Columbus Ave where I knew I could easily get a cab. About 20 minutes later the cab dropped me on Fifth

Avenue and I walked quickly through to the ornate gates near the entrance to the Zoo.

Cyran was already there, even though I was early, standing off to the side of the path looking at his phone. He was wearing jeans, another t-shirt but a blue one this time and on his head he had a blue baseball cap. Seems like we had both been on the same page about suitable clothing for a zoo date. Cyran was also carrying the same quite large backpack he had with him when he visited me on campus earlier in the week, which seemed a bit bigger than necessary for a day in Central Park.

Reaching where Cyran was standing, I greeted him with a "Hello Curtis" to get his attention. It felt very strange calling him by that name, but I supposed I needed to get used to it. As Cyran looked up from his phone, his face broke into smile. "Hi Dr Lucy, it's great to see you. Is it okay if I give you a hug hello?"

I certainly had no objections to the idea of a hug, and I was touched by his politeness. The six or so inches of height he had on me meant that he had to bend down just a little to wrap his arms around me as he dropped a gentle peck of a kiss on my check. He felt warm and strong and very safe.

"I hope you haven't been waiting too long?" I asked Cyran as we broke apart. "It's only just 10 now, I thought I would be here earlier, but New York traffic is predictably bad even on Saturday."

"The traffic was fine for me," Cyran said with a hint of laughter in his voice. "I was early just because I wanted to make extra sure I was here before you, so you were not waiting around. I thought that might make you anxious about whether I was going to turn up."

"I am very glad you are here, that you did turn up, thank you. This would have been a boring day without you," I admitted. "Are you ready to get our day started? I checked the schedule on the website and there is a penguin feeding at 10.40am if we want to see that. Also, if we want coffee, which I most definitely do, we should get that on the way in."

"Sounds great, both the coffee and the penguins."

I had bought tickets online this morning so that we would not need to wait or queue to get in. I ushered Cyran through the ornate gates and we turned left into the Zoo's cafe. Ten minutes later, with large lattes in hand, we entered the Zoo proper.

Cyran had originally taken his latte in his right hand but swapped it to his left as we walked. With his right side now free, he reached down to hold my left hand, gently asking me if that was okay as he did so. I gave my consent through a strong grip on his hand and said, "That would be lovely." Somewhat spoiling the tender moment, I continued, "I used to come here all the time with my dad when I was a kid, and when I was really little, he always held my hand too, but for different reasons."

Cyran laughed. "I'm not worried about you running off and getting lost Dr Lucy. But I do like having you close." I liked having him close too.

Walking through the park, our first stop was to see the sea lions basking in the sun in their octagonal habitat in the central garden area. We then kept walking along the paved walkways, determined to keep holding hands as we dodged families with prams and tourists taking photos, and eventually reached the penguins with about 10 minutes to spare before the feeding session.

As we waited, Cyran picked up on what I had said earlier. "You said you used to come here as a kid, has it changed much since then?"

"Not a huge amount it seems, although I haven't been back for quite a few years. The key difference is that when I was younger the polar bear Gus was still alive, and I loved visiting him and watching him swim."

"There was a polar bear here in New York?" Cyran seemed very surprised.

"Yes, for many years. Gus died in his late 20s I think, so he was a major drawcard for the Zoo for a very long time, but I did wonder as a kid whether he was very lonely all by himself. Now we have a grizzly bear and of course the sea lions and lots of penguins."

The penguin feeding and keeper talk that went with it was excellent and very interesting. Even better was the fact that while we were standing in the crowd listening, Cyran had slipped around behind me and hugged me close from behind. Our heads were close together side by side and I could feel his warm breath on my cheek as I was trying to pay attention to the penguin keeper.

After visiting the penguins, we spent the next hour or so walking, looking at the animals and chatting casually. Cyran held my hand the whole time, like he didn't want to let me go, but in a supportive way not a possessive way. Shortly after noon my stomach had started growling, prompting a discussion whether we should get some quick and easy take out from the Zoo's café or find somewhere outside the park that was a bit fancier.

"Well, I'm really hungry so I think we need to eat here," Cyran said decisively, and we headed back to the Zoo entrance. The café had many black wire picnic style tables set up outside, some under a pergola and others out in the courtyard getting the direct sun. It was busy, but there were enough free tables that we had our pick of locations.

"You bought the last lunch so let me organise this one,"

Cyran offered. "How about you find somewhere to sit, and I will go and get us some food. Any allergies, likes or dislikes I should know about?"

"I would like something warm please. A burger with fries and a lemonade would be good. I am sure that they will have all of that." Then thinking that Cyran would have his hands full when he returned, I offered, "Do you want me to mind your backpack while you get the food?"

"Nope. Thanks, but it needs to stay with me at all times," Cyran responded. "My other clothes, my work clothes are in here."

I felt slightly foolish that it had not occurred to me before about the contents of Cyran's backpack and why he always carried it. Of course, he would need instant access to his flight suit in case of an emergency.

While Cyran went inside the building, with his backpack firmly on his shoulder, I found us a table outside in the sunshine. Cyran was back just a few minutes later with a tray piled high with food. There seemed to be about four burgers, some nachos and several pieces of pizza, and two very large cups of fries.

"I got a bit of everything. That way if you don't like the burger there is plenty to choose from."

Conscious of Cyran's request on our previous date that he didn't want to talk his alien identity in public, I lowered my voice and asked discretely, "I know I'm not supposed to ask you questions about this sort of thing, but do you have a large appetite or did you just over order?" I waved my hand over the overloaded tray on the table. "Is all this something to do with your *job*?"

Cyran grabbed a fry and ducked it in the small cardboard pot of ketchup on the tray. He didn't look cross or offended by my question. "It's okay to ask, and yes, I need to eat a great deal of food, mostly because of where I was born," he explained. "When I was a teenager, my mother used to complain that I ate more than the rest of the family combined. These days I still burn a lot of calories, particularly when I am active in my job and regularly 'commuting' like getting here this morning."

"Commuting? Is that what you call it?" I asked with a laugh, thinking that only Cyran could compare flying across the Atlantic to catching a bus. "I suppose that works in this context."

"Well, I'll have you know my skills at commuting are very useful. I get to come to New York, and hang out with penguins and pretty scientists, and eat many many burgers," Cyran joked. "And unlike these pretty scientists I only have one university degree, so I have to make a living somehow."

My curiosity spiked, and I was bubbling with more questions, but not sure what I could ask without being impolite. My first question was, "So do you get paid for what you do?"

"No, I don't, actually. Seems a bit off to me to take money for helping people. Sorry I was joking about that. I have royalty rights from several patents based on my first family's tech and that keeps me in burgers and pays my bills. Means I can avoid working a 9-to-5 job, which would hamper my ability to do my other job."

Still curious, I followed up with another less controversial question. "You mentioned Oxford the other day, did you study there?"

"Yes, I did. I studied a Bachelor of Arts majoring in History and Politics. I was interested in humanities and social sciences subjects, not so much with the maths and science like you."

"After university I went to work immediately for the

Government." Cyran looked sheepishly at me. "But I can't talk about that sorry, too many national security laws, secrets etc etc. It very quickly became too difficult for me to be officially tied to the UK Government." He sighed as he continued, "Well too difficult for various government people, who made it too difficult for me. So I took some time off for a while, and then I decided I was going to go effectively freelance. And here I am today doing what I do." He waved his hands in a 'look at me' gesture.

"Well, I am certainly glad of all that, otherwise we would not have met."

As we chatted Cyran was very casually but consistently working his way through the pile of food he had brought to the table. I ate one of the burgers and some fries, and then just sat and sipped my drink as he kept going, trying not to be too amazed about how much he was managing to consume in one meal.

"So, tell me about your family?" Cyran asked me. "Who is the birthday party for today?"

"My niece, Mia, who turned six yesterday. She is my sister Gabriela's daughter. We are having a party at a play place for her school friends and then family dinner tonight at my parents' house with the whole family. All my brothers are married and two of them have kids as well. There are eighteen of us in total so it gets a bit loud and crazy when we are all together. But I do love them all."

"That's very different to my family, there are only four of us adults and my sister's twins. Beth's partner bailed on her when she got pregnant, claiming he was too young at 26 to be a dad. Total loser really."

"That's awful. Are you guys close?"

"Yes, Beth and I are close. As I think I mentioned last time, she is a teacher, and lives in a small village about an hour and half outside London. She moved there for a better life with the kids, particularly as she is by herself still. About three years ago when Dad retired, Mum and Dad moved up to the same village so they could be close to her and the kids. I go up there regularly to see them all. It's very easy on the train or of course by other forms of commuting." Cyran did air quotes with his fingers around the word commuting.

"Right, let's go for a walk and let someone else have the table," Cyran suggested suddenly, which I took to mean he was finished eating. He stood up, grabbed his backpack from where it had been sitting on the ground between his feet and offered his hand to me as I also stood up.

We headed out, holding hands as we walked through one of the three archways out of the Zoo and into the main park and headed north on the path under the East 65th St bridge.

We spent the next hour or so meandering along the paths of the east side of Central Park, stopping to comment on interesting flower beds, rock formations and statues. Our conversation was light and effortless. The afternoon was getting warm, and by the time we reached Pilgrim Hill, I was feeling hot and bothered. We stopped in the shade to have a drink, and I checked my watch. It was nearly 2pm.

"What time do you need to leave for this party?" Cyran queried. "Do we need to head out to the street so you can grab a cab?"

"Pretty soon, sorry. The kids party starts at 4pm, so I need to leave here by 2pm to get home first and then out to Queens."

Cyran stopped walking and leaned in towards me reassuringly. "Don't be sorry, I knew you had other things to do today, and I am just glad you could fit me in. I have really enjoyed it." Still holding my hand, he turned towards me so we were facing each other and asked, "Can I call you or text you to organise another opportunity to see you? I would like to take you out to dinner sometime soon, or a movie perhaps?"

"Yes please." My response was simple but heartfelt. "I would very much like to do something again soon. I am free most evenings and the next few weekends, but after that I will be away for a week or so at a conference in the first week of June. A real one not a secret NASA taskforce."

Cyran laughed. "Okay that all sounds great, my schedule is a bit unpredictable, but I will be in touch."

When we reached Fifth Avenue a few minutes later, I suddenly I felt self-conscious for the first time in our day together, not knowing the most appropriate way to end the date. Cyran must have sensed my anxiety spike, so swept me up into a hug and lightly pecked my cheek with his lips. "Have a lovely afternoon, and I will talk to you soon Dr Lucy. I had a great day." With the ease of local New Yorker, Cyran stepped off the sidewalk and hailed a passing cab, hugging me again gently as he ushered me into it. "See you soon and thank you."

Chapter 11
Cyran

Despite ending our day at the Zoo with plans to spend lots more time together, it was nearly two weeks later before I got my next proper date with Lucy.

On Sunday morning after our date, I took a yoga class at a studio near home and then waited impatiently until it was late enough in New York for me text Lucy good morning without waking her up. We made plans for dinner Tuesday night at a new Italian restaurant that Lucy had apparently been meaning to try. Lucy later reassured she had really enjoyed her pasta as she sat in the restaurant alone waiting for me while I was in Korea.

On Thursday we managed a quick coffee in Boston, literally 15 minutes squeezed in between meetings for Lucy and cut short by me getting a call out to a train derailment in Germany. We had tentative plans to do something together on Sunday, but this did not eventuate as I spent all weekend in Chile helping with search and rescue after a massive avalanche near a ski resort in the Andes.

Lucy seemed to be understanding of it all, but I was frustrated that I was having a busy period just when I wanted to spend whatever time I could with Lucy. We had got into a routine of texting to keep in touch throughout the day and often talking on the phone at night. The four-hour time difference between London and New York was manageable as I was usually up very late.

Our casual texting and chatting were a good way to learn about each other's day to day lives and get to know each other a little better. I was very comfortable talking to Lucy about both the mundane things of my life as a regular guy and my adventures across the world helping people out.

I discovered that the conference Lucy had mentioned was she was attending in early June was an international physics symposium at Oxford. She had admitted in one of our late-night conversations that she was one of the keynote speakers at the event and was currently working with her research team to get their data ready for an extensive presentation. I was amazed about how much she seemed to juggle in her work life, with two university jobs, plus her role at Bright Eco-electricity, although I didn't really understand quite how she was involved with that company.

The following Tuesday we made plans for lunch at the Thai Place near campus in New York, thinking a repeat of our first lunch date might work well. I was getting ready to head across the Atlantic when I got a call from the Prime Minister's office about a major incident in Yorkshire (involving a tunnel, a lorry carrying toxic material and a bus load of school students). I left home immediately to see what I could do to help.

When I arrived at the site of the crash it was soon evident that this was not a fix and run type scenario where I could be done in a few minutes. The lorry was tilted sideways and wedged tightly in the tunnel and green goo was leaking out of several of the tanks on the back of the truck. I sighed as I realised that, damn it, I was going to miss yet another date with Lucy.

There was about a dozen cars now at a standstill on the road heading towards the tunnel, and some the drivers were arguing with the police about the emergency services vehicles which had blocked them in. Others were taking photos and filming the scene on their mobile phones.

After I touched down, my first task was to speak to the incident commander on site, who was from the Yorkshire Fire and Rescue Service. She shook my hand and said, "Thank you for coming Cyran. Can you wait just a moment while my team finishes the site assessment? We have a drone in the tunnel getting footage and this will enable us to determine the best course of action. Then we will get you helping."

Happy to comply, I took a couple of steps back out of the commander's way to let her work. Then conscious that I was about to stand Lucy up yet again, I did something that was not in my normal rule book for Cyran behaviour. I had both my phones stashed in the deep pockets on the side of my flight suit, and so I took a moment to reach for my personal phone and send a quick text to Lucy.

> Not going to make it sorry.

What I hadn't noticed was that some of the people standing around had turned their phones towards me and were taking photos of what I was doing.

Coffee with a Superhero

A couple of hours later, the spill was mostly cleaned up, the lorry removed from the tunnel and the school children safe. I was filthy, with road dirt and splashes of the toxic spill on my clothes. Before I left the scene, I touched base with the incident commander who thanked me once again but would not shake my hand this time as she had just seen me elbow deep in a tank of toxic waste. Fair enough really.

It was another hour before I realised how much trouble I had got myself in with text I had sent to Lucy. I had got home and showered, grabbed some food from the takeaway on the corner, and plonked down on the sofa to eat it before I saw the message from my sister Beth.

> BETH
>
> So, you've gone totally viral, who were you texting?

Puzzled, I typed my name into the search engine on my phone and discovered the entire internet seemed to have gone crazy over a photo of me taken at the crash site in Yorkshire.

There I was in my flight suit, my personal phone in its bright purple case in my hand, sending the text to Lucy. Thankfully only back of the phone was visible, not the screen, so there was no chance of anyone working out who I had been texting. The phone case itself could be clearly identified, and I was disappointed that I would now have to replace it with something new.

There were news articles about the photo, social media commentary and already several videos discussing my 'actions'. Some of the comments were hate filled, focused on how I should have been helping not spending time on my phone, and many were just speculating on what exactly I was doing. Suggestions ranged from contacting my evil alien overlords to sending heart emojis to the American pop star currently touring in the UK.

The Prime Minister had even been asked for his views about my actions during a press conference at the opening of a new train station. Thankfully he simply said that the Government appreciated my help with the incident and that he was not going to comment on anything relating to my personal life.

My football club, London FC, whose logo was on my phone case, also seemed to be taking it well. Their social media team was probably thrilled about the free publicity and had issued a statement saying that they appreciated my support of their fabulous club.

News and social media commentary about my super-hero actions was business as usual, and I was usually pretty good at just ignoring all the chatter and all the haters. This seemed different somehow, and even more petty than normal. I dropped my now world-famous phone onto the sofa and just held my head in my hands for a while, frustrated that a simple act of courtesy had turned into something this ridiculous.

Needing to have a vent, I called Beth, but the call went to her voicemail. I then rang Lucy and got her recorded voice asking me to leave a message, which was not surprising given it was still business hours in New York. I told her voicemail that I would ring her later.

I followed up with a quick text message to Beth that just let her know I was okay, but I did not want to put any details in a text on the off chance her phone was seen by the kids or someone outside the family. Beth's twins were nine years old, so a little young yet for social media, and they didn't know about my secret identity.

I also thought about calling Mum, but she probably had no idea what was going on unless Beth had let her know. My parents still got most of their news from the BBC nightly broadcast or the morning paper, and hopefully the BBC was sensible enough to not cover this non-story. Also, unfortunately there would probably not be a lot of sympathy coming from my parents about my ridiculous burst of internet fame. It was more likely going to be a well-mannered, "I told you so." Mum in particular had been quite firm a few years back when I started using my alien abilities in a public way that she was worried it was a bad idea, and that I should be focused on living a quiet normal life. The whole world talking about who I was texting was the sort of thing my parents had been worried about.

So instead, I spent the evening moping around at home, eating a lot of pizza and watching home renovation shows.

A few days later I did get to see Lucy in person, but this was most definitely not a date. Director Malone from NASA had reconvened the comet taskforce for an update meeting in Washington on Friday, having given us a few days' notice this time.

The media spotlight on me and my text message had only lasted 48 hours. Thankfully a Hollywood power couple had announced their engagement, and the world was talking about that now instead of speculating about my telecommunications habits.

On Friday morning we had a 9am start time for the task-force meeting, to give those on the East Coast a chance to fly into Washington that morning. The later start was also necessary for the participants on the West Coast of the US, most of whom were joining us online via a secure link. The scientists in other countries also got to join online, with time zones meaning that it is the middle of the night for some of them.

Lucy had arrived before me, and she was deep in conversation with a group of the other scientists when I landed in the courtyard outside the conference room. We had spoken briefly on the phone last night, joking about how today we would need to pretend we were still only professional acquaintances. I did ask Lucy for her preferred lunch order though, on the assumption that we would be supplied terrible sandwiches again. Pasta was on the menu today.

At the mid-morning coffee break I was determined to speak to Lucy. I was once again seated at the top of the table, and I initially got caught up in some brief chit chat with Director Malone and Oran Coombes from the White House who was also attending the meeting today. When they got up to get coffee, I made my way over to where Lucy was standing near the doorway to the courtyard. She was holding a cookie in one hand and juggling a bottle of water and her phone in the other.

"Good morning, Dr Cortez," I said formally as I arrived beside her. "It is a pleasure to see you here. I trust you have been keeping well since I saw you last."

Lucy's eyes danced with laughter as she matched my tone. "Hello Mr Cyran. It is a pleasure to see you too, and yes, I have been very well since our last meeting." Dropping her voice to a conspiratorial whisper, she asked, "Why are we suddenly talking like we are in a Jane Austen novel?"

My undignified snort of laughter in response to Lucy's question drew the attention of several of the nearby taskforce members who turned to look at us. So much for pretending we were just professional acquaintances. Thank goodness everyone in the room was bound by a million national security requirements and no-one would be posting about this conversation on the internet.

All too soon it was back to the meeting. Once again, I enjoyed watching Lucy in action today, engaging in intense discussions about all sorts of science related things I did not really understand. Late morning Director Malone directed us into breakout sessions focussed on our individual aspects of the project. Lucy gathered outside in the courtyard with the NASA personnel and other rocket scientists, and I was with the Director huddled around a laptop talking with some of those online about the diplomatic and logistical issues communicating to the world about the comet's arrival.

Our lunch break, when it finally came, was pretty much a repeat of the days of the original taskforce gathering a few weeks ago. I knew what Lucy wanted food-wise, so I left the NASA building as soon as I could, and was back twenty minutes later, delivering her a spaghetti carbonara. Lucy was sitting outside in the courtyard waiting for me to arrive. The spring weather was warmer than it was for our previous week of taskforce meetings, so there were more people in the courtyard today, with several small groups at the tables or standing around soaking up what sunshine made it into the courtyard.

"Sorry, that took longer than I expected," I said after I sat down across from her at one of the outdoor tables. "But it is still very warm."

"Thank you," Lucy said. "I am hungry, so it won't take me long to eat this, it smells delicious."

"Good. Hey, as much as I would like to sit and chat you now, I think I better go and do some networking. But quickly, when are you heading back?" I asked very quietly. "Are you staying over in Washington tonight or going home?"

Lucy raised her hands and shoulders in a shrug. "I am not sure yet, I haven't booked anything in terms of a hotel here or a flight home. I will fly out either tonight or first thing in the morning. But if you are around, it would be nice to catch up. We still haven't talked about that crazy phone thing that's going on."

At that moment I noticed that Director Malone was heading out into the courtyard, looking towards where we were sitting. "Enjoy your meal Dr Lucy," I said, as I stood up. I turned towards the Director as she approached us and gave her my best professional smile, mentally flicking a more formal mask back on.

"Sorry to interrupt you both," Director Malone said warmly. "Dr Cortez, I am sorry the food hasn't been to your liking at these meetings, but I am glad to see you have been well looked after by Cyran here."

"No problem at all," Lucy replied to the Director, matching her friendly tone. "It has all worked out quite well and given Cyran and I an opportunity to get to know each other." I was a little surprised by how honest Lucy was being, but I suppose there was no point in hiding the obvious fact that I had been paying special attention to her.

"Well, that's good." Turning to me, Director Malone continued, "Cyran I need your help again with a translation. When you are finished here, can you come across to the table?" And with that request it was back to work for me, and back to finishing her lunch alone for Lucy.

Coffee with a Superhero

The taskforce meeting was finished shortly before 4pm. Although I was not 100 percent following some of technical details of the discussions, it was obvious everyone was pleased with the progress that had been made today and in recent weeks. We finished the day by formalising a plan to have relevant discussions online as needed over the next few weeks while work on building the satellites and the rockets to take them into orbit continued.

As everyone gathered up their belongings, I looked over towards where Lucy remained seated at the table, typing on her laptop. Right at that moment my personal phone vibrated with an incoming message, so I walked across the room out to the courtyard to get some privacy and grabbed my phone from the pocket of my flight suit.

The incoming message was from Lucy, who was sitting only about 20 feet away from me.

DR LUCY

I'm texting to keep this private. Do you want to have dinner in New York a bit later? If I leave now, I will be there around 7pm. Another try at the Italian place on W 84th? The food was amazingly good last time I was there.

Sounds great. Text me when you are ready and I will meet you there.

DR LUCY

Good plan. No emergencies please! I want to see you and actually talk to you.

I will do my best. See you soon C xxx

I did make it to dinner although I was about 10 minutes

late after a quick trip to Uruguay and an even quicker stop at home to grab some smart clothes appropriate for dinner in an Upper West Side restaurant. Lucy was waiting for me at the bar when I arrived, and after I had kissed her cheek and apologised for being late, we were quickly seated in a cosy table tucked into a bay window overlooking the street.

Once the waiter had left us, the first thing Lucy asked me very cheekily was, "So how's your week been then, seen any good social media posts?"

I banged the menu I was holding into my forehead. "I can't believe all the beat up. It was one text message that took fifteen seconds. People need to focus on more important things."

"I wasn't sure whether to laugh or cry about it all really. I was very sorry you had to put up with that rubbish."

"Are you going to ask me the obvious question?" I probed. "Because the answer is yes, it was you."

Lucy laughed. "I wasn't going to ask, because I had figured that was the case. I do feel very special though, that you went through all that to let me know you were not going to make it to lunch."

Switching from laughter to a more concerned tone, Lucy continued, "How are you feeling about the whole phone incident, now that it seems to be over?"

"I'm fine, thanks, but not really something I want to talk about here," I replied, gesturing around the room to remind Lucy we were in a very public place.

While I had told Lucy I was fine, I was not sure that was totally true. It had been three days now and I was still angry about the violation of my privacy. This level of scrutiny on a personal moment and the amount of fuss it had generated seems absurd. I had known going into this line of work that using my abilities in a public role would mean significant media and internet attention. But perhaps naively I had thought the focus would be on my work.

I was also really cross that I had to buy a new phone case as this one had been a gift from my sister. I had hidden the internet famous London FC phone case at the back of a drawer at home and bought a new very nondescript black case.

Pushing my angry thoughts aside, I focused on enjoying Lucy's company and enjoying our meal. Lucy was right, the food here was amazing, and I had quick stab of guilt that I had not made it to our previous date last week.

As we ate our dessert, which for me was an incredible tiramisu and for Lucy a panna cotta served very artfully in a flat champagne coupe glass, Lucy raised the topic of her upcoming trip to the UK for the physics conference.

After giving me a quick overview of her schedule for the conference itself, Lucy moved on to her plans for the weekend after the event. "We finish on a Thursday night, and I was thinking about coming down to London for Friday and Saturday to spend some time with you if that suits. I will get myself a hotel somewhere central, and I was hoping you could take me sightseeing? It would be great to have a local tour guide."

I really liked that idea and I was happy to do anything Lucy wanted. Hopefully we could have two full days together without work interruptions.

"That would be fabulous to spend some time together in London," I confirmed. "I am free anytime that weekend, except for my friend Dev's birthday dinner on the Friday night. I would love to take you with me to that as my date if you are okay with meeting my friends?" Lucy looked briefly concerned at that idea, so I continued quickly, "No pressure, if you are not comfortable with that, I will tell them I am busy and just take you out to dinner instead."

"It's fine, I think that will nice, I would like to get to know your friends. My first reaction to new social situations is always a bit of panic though, sorry."

"Great, it's a date - a weekend long date."

Chapter 12
Lucy

The second weekend of June I flew to London to attend the physics symposium. The previous two weeks had gone past very quickly as I had been hyper focussed on preparing for my presentation and working with my team to ensure our research was perfect.

By Thursday evening, after three days of presentations, breakout discussions and some polite scientific debates, the event was finally over. I had an early dinner with some chatty Australians working at the Square Kilometre Array telescopes in the remote outback in Western Australia. Then my car service whisked me down the M1 motorway into the noise and bustle of London, where I was staying at a very private boutique hotel on Park Lane.

My flight home was not until Sunday morning, so I was looking forward to having two completely free days to spend with Cyran playing tourist in London. No natural disasters, wars or other catastrophic events that needed him dare interfere!

On Friday morning I was still in bed drinking coffee when my phone rang. It was Cyran. "Good morning, Dr Lucy - how is my hometown treating you so far? And are you ready for a day of exploring?" Was I imagining it or did Cyran's accent seemed broader this morning, more British than ever?

"In order, good morning to you to, yes London is treating me well so far, and I am very excited about seeing everything you want to show me. But I am not actually ready, currently still in bed."

"Unfortunately, it's not going to be possible to see every-thing. It's a big city with nearly 2000 years of history," Cyran said. "But let's start with breakfast and then head out on foot to Buckingham Palace if you like. The weather is looking good, it's cool but clear and won't rain today. I want to take you to all the super touristy places first, the Palace, Trafalgar Square, the London Eye and of course Big Ben."

"Absolutely," I agreed. I had been to London several times before but only for quick work or study related trips, not to be a tourist. "But a shower and food first. Where are you and when can you get here?"

Cyran laughed. "Still not used to the fact that I can get anywhere anytime? I am currently at my flat, which is about 20 mins away from you on the Tube or 20 seconds away if I fly, so I can meet you whenever you like." Twenty seconds was a bit soon, as I did need a shower to fully wake me up, so we agreed to meet in the hotel lobby in 30 minutes.

Cyran was waiting when I went downstairs 29 minutes later, sitting on a couch in the lobby. He was looked very handsome today, wearing jeans, a camel-coloured casual button-down shirt and his leather coat. His signature hair was up in a sexy mess of a man-bun, and his eyes were blue, as he was in Curtis mode, not Cyran mode.

"Good morning, Curtis." I called as a crossed the foyer and casually touched his arm. He had his chunky phone in his hand, which looked more like a radio than a regular smart phone. As he looked up from the phone there was fleeting glint of concern in his warm blue eyes for just a second.

"Good morning yourself ma'am," he said, doing an over exaggerated British accent. "Ready for a hearty English breakfast and then a hearty English tourism day?"

"Yes, totally ready for both - but is everything okay? You looked concerned." '

Cyran sighed. "Nothing I need to deal with right now certainly. Just a heads up about a potential work thing that might be developing. Let's eat."

The hotel's dining room was quiet, as anyone staying here on business would have long been and gone. Cyran and I laughed and chatted over Eggs Benedict and fancy pots of tea. I told him about the Australian scientists I had met in Oxford who lived 300 kilometres from the nearest town and were desperate for good coffee, and he told me in a whisper about the work he had done in Botswana over the weekend.

We lingered over for nearly an hour before Cyran started to fidget and look ready to move on with the day.

"Okay, formal tourist date planning time," Cyran said. "I suggest we do Buckingham Palace first, as it is about a 15-minute walk from here, but we can grab a cab if you don't want to walk. Although if we do walk, we can visit the Bomber Command Memorial on the way past. It's right at the end of the street, and you might find that interesting."

"A walk sounds good to me," I said. "Let's do it."

When we left the hotel, we headed down Park Lane, across Piccadilly and into the west side of the Green Park. Cyran had obviously done some tour guide homework and explained to me that the park was one of the eight Royal Parks in London and had been created in 1660 by King Charles II.

Our first stop was the poignant Bomber Command Memorial. It honoured the courage and sacrifice of the airmen of Britain and other nations who flew with the Royal Air Force during World War II as part of Bomber Command, flying through the dark night after night to undertake bombing raids across Germany.

Heading into the heart of the park, we strolled through the beautiful green space around to the Queen Victoria Memorial in front of the entrance to Buckingham Palace. As we walked, Cyran took my hand in his, and my skin fizzled and my heart fluttered at his warmth.

When we reached Buckingham Palace, I unfortunately had to drop Cyran's hand so that I could take way too many photos of the iconic black and gold gates with the Palace behind them, jostling with thousands of other tourists for the best angles of the famous building.

We filled the morning with a whirl of visiting amazingly famous sights, warm relaxed conversation and enjoying a sunny day. We walked down The Mall, through the Admiralty Arch, said hello to the lions in Trafalgar Square and took a selfie together in front of Nelson's column.

"My feet are getting sore," I told Cyran as we stood in Trafalgar Square, watching both people and pigeons go about their day. "Even though I have been amazed at how close together all these key places actually are to one another, and how much we have seen so far, my feet are complaining. Not me, just to clarify, only my feet."

"Sorry to hear that. Score out of ten for the tour so far?" Cyran asked jokingly.

I tilted my head thoughtfully. "Nine out of ten for the tour, ten out of ten for the tour guide."

"Why only nine out of ten?"

"Well, I deducted a point as the tour needs more stops for coffee, and probably for lunch. Not all of us have infinite stamina you know."

After Cyran had apologised profusely for keeping me from my coffee, we headed out of the square found a little cafe just down one of the many side streets. The cafe had a few small tables out the front that were full, but inside it was much less crowded, and we were able to pick a quiet table in the corner to give us some privacy.

Once we were seated, Cyran leaned forward with the menu in his hands and whispered to me. "Just let me make sure the menu is safe first before we commit to eating here, free of horrible sandwiches or other cold food or anything featuring mustard."

I smiled, pleased that he was being kind and charming about my not-so-secret sensitivities around eating cold food. "I'm okay with them being on the menu," I whispered back. "Just not the only thing on the menu."

He leaned back and laughed loudly. I reached out and touched his arm, "Shush. Do not draw the attention of the sandwich loving public."

After lunch, which featured a delightfully warm chicken burger and a discussion about why America called deep fried potatoes fries and Britain called them chips, we set out exploring again. Heading in a south-easterly direction, we walked past the gated entrance to Downing Street and giggled about tourists trying to get a photo of the Prime Minister's residence without being glared at by security.

The next stop was across the road from Big Ben to admire the giant clock on the Houses of Parliament and take another selfie, and then we walked across Westminster Bridge towards the London Eye.

As we walked along the embankment on the side of the river, Cyran leaned in closely and said in a whisper, "Did you know that on JandaKo there are no bodies of water larger that the width of the Thames? We had lots of rivers that ran from hills to underground water basins, but no seas. Seas still freak me out a bit."

"How much do you remember of your home?" I asked quietly. "Is it hard to remember your time before the trip? Sorry I don't remember how old you were when you left."

"That's alright, I don't expect you to have memorised my backstory. I was basically the same age as I was when I arrived - eight years old. Well, I was about eight biological years when I arrived, I don't know exactly how long I was asleep on the ship."

"I do remember quite a lot," Cyran continued. "I think about as much as any adult remembers of their first eight years of life. Snippets and vague memories of things, a lot of colours and smells and emotions. Some things, like my older brother's laugh stand out very clearly. Certain events I remember well, like playing in the purple forest." He sighed, the sadness clear in his eyes as he thought of his first family. "Sorry, it was so long ago, but I still miss them." He turned away.

"Don't apologise!" It was not clear if he was sorry for talking about them or for feeling sad, but neither was something to be sorry about.

"You can talk to me about your family, and of course about your feelings." I turned and hugged him tight. He was very warm, and his arms wrapped around me as he leaned into the hug.

"Thank you, that means a lot to me." Cyran's voice was slightly ragged, filled with emotion he didn't quite know what to do with. Still with his arms hugging me tight but trying to lighten the mood he said with a light laugh, "But of course I am British, and we don't do feelings as much as you Americans."

We were in public, on the stone paved walkway along the banks of the Thames with tourists and locals swarming around us, but I wanted that hug to never end. I felt safe in his arms.

Cyran reached a hand up to my face and gently cupped my jaw. I looked up at him, and his face now looked much more serious than a moment ago. "I would very much like to kiss you now," he whispered gently, as if the question was secret and sacred. "Would that be okay?"

I was touched that consent was so important to Cyran. "Yes, please. That would be very nice." Cyran lent downward. I looked up, and our eyes met, and then our lips met, our mouths luxuriating in the feel and taste of each other as we came together.

No doubt conscious that we were in a public place, Cyran gently broke the kiss a few moments later, despite me wanting this moment to never end. "Thank you," I said, feeling that that was a wholly inadequate response but not knowing what else to say after such an epic first kiss.

"No, thank you," Cyran murmured as he reached down and took my hand. "You okay to keep walking or do you need a minute?"

I reassured Cyran I was good to go, so we stated walking again, holding hands and strolling along the river. Soon afterwards though, my energy levels plummeted, and I told

Cyran that I needed a rest and maybe yet another coffee. As I pulled out my phone to search for nearby cafe, Cyran said "I pretty sure there's a good one..."

But then he paused mid-sentence and raised his eyebrows with a serious look on his face. Cyran pulled his chunky phone out of one of his pockets and glanced at the screen quickly. Turning sideways to face me, his hand lifted to touch my face softly as he stepped backwards. "Sorry, got to run."

He sprinted off down a side road, at a speed that was only just not too fast for a man to be casually running down a London street. At the first corner he turned and was gone.

I sighed, thinking we needed a protocol for this sort of thing. It was all very well him dashing off to save someone, assuming that was what he was doing not just suddenly remembering to pick up his dry cleaning, but I wondered what I was supposed to do now? Should I wait? Get a taxi and go back to the hotel? Find a nearby cafe and check the news websites and socials to see where he was and who he was rescuing from what?

I felt deflated that my fabulous date had just ended very abruptly and it was hard not to feel a bit grumpy about being abandoned. Go back to the hotel, I decided. My feet were sore, and there was a giant bathtub in my hotel room I could use to have a nice long soak to ease my tired feet and legs. I texted Cyran to let him know what I was doing. I knew he carried his phone with him when he was working, but I didn't expect he would see my message until he was finished whatever he was currently doing.

Coffee with a Superhero

I was heading down the hotel corridor towards my room when my phone chirped in my bag with an incoming text. I grabbed my phone out only to be disappointed the message was from Kane and not from Cyran.

I had been keeping Kane up to date when we saw each other at work on Wednesdays, and via regular phone chats, with the ongoing developments in my relationship with Cyran. He knew that we were sightseeing together today in London and was obviously keen for any gossip.

KANE

Soooooo, updates please! - how's it all going?

Give me five and I will call you.

A few minutes later I had freshened up a bit, poured myself a sparkling water from the mini-bar and was ready to report in to my best friend. I slipped my headphones into my ears, dialled, and Kane answered on the first ring.

"Hey Lucy, tell me all the news! How was the date with Mr Darcy? Are you still on the date?"

"Firstly, that's not his name, it's Curtis, and secondly, well no I am not still on the date. It ended suddenly unfortunately because Curtis had a work emergency. Now I am back at the hotel with sore feet." My disappointment with how the day ended was making me grumpy, but I didn't want to take it out on Kane.

"Oh dear, you sound grumpy. That's not good. I don't mean to sound offensive, but was this a real work emergency that Curtis had, or the type you fake to get out of a terrible date that's not going well?" Kane laughed as he continued, "I've done that more than a few times."

"Definitely a real emergency, and as Curtis had kissed

me for the first time not long before he had to take off, I think the date was going well."

"Ooh that does sound like good news. Tell me, how was it, is he a good kisser?"

"It was lovely, and that's all I am going to say. You might be my best friend, Kane, but you don't get all the details. Anyway, shouldn't you be working?"

"Ha, perks of being the CEO. I get to make personal phone calls about my friends' romantic life anytime I want to. And don't forget you rang me."

"That's true," I admitted. "How about you go back to work, and I go have a bath? I have sore legs and feet, and I need some down time before dinner. Curtis and I have plans to go out to dinner with his friends, assuming his work stuff gets sorted."

"Keep me posted and enjoy the bath. I hope you make it out to dinner and that his friends are not all strange English serial killers."

On that sober note our conversation ended. I headed for the bathroom, armed with my Kindle and my drink, and sank into a very large bubble bath to blot out the world for a while.

Chapter 13
Cyran

As we had walked along the embankment by the river, my satellite phone had vibrated and beeped quietly in my pocket with an incoming emergency notification. It was a tornado warning for Oklahoma with reports of a twister touching down near a small rural community.

It was just over an hour later when I was finished in Oklahoma and was ready to head back to London. I was covered in small flecks of dirt and what looked like corn. I desperately needed a shower and would need to put a new set of contact lenses in my eyes, so I looked human again before I went out in public.

Landing on the rooftop terrace of my flat, I let myself in and headed for the kitchen in search of some food to keep me going until dinner. When I pulled my personal phone out of my backpack, I found a message from Lucy letting me know she was heading back to her hotel. She had sent it only a few minutes after I had left London, so she would well and truly back at the hotel by now.

I stared at my phone briefly. I was a bit apprehensive

about checking in with Lucy after I had run out on her in the middle of our date. Today had been the first real example of how my work was going to impact our relationship. At least I didn't have to lie to Lucy about where I had been.

Lucy picked up quickly when I rang, as if she was holding her phone. "Hello, fly boy, where are you now?" Her tone was upbeat, with no trace of anger. "I am back at the hotel, having a bath to soak my tired legs and feet from all that walking."

"Good to hear. I am back in London, and I just got to my flat. I have Oklahoma corn and dirt in my hair from wrestling a tornado."

"Is everyone alright? Did you get there in time to help?"

"Yes, we got everyone into the shelters. I was able to divert the twister slightly, so it didn't hit the town straight on and so there was only minor damage. Really scary for the school kids though, as there was a large regional school on the edge of town."

"Well done, that's excellent news."

"I am really sorry that I needed to leave you on your own in the middle of London." I cautiously injected a little laughter into my voice. "Occupational hazard I am afraid."

Lucy's response was quick and firm. "Firstly, please do not apologise for doing your job, your majorly important job. I was a bit unsure about what I was supposed to do and whether to wait at first, but I am completely fine. We just need to work out some more date parameters around what I should do when you suddenly need to disappear off to Oklahoma or anywhere else."

Thankfully, it seemed Lucy wasn't angry with me or the situation. Before I could say anything else, Lucy continued, "But secondly, you are interrupting my bath, and it sounds like you need a shower. How about we finish this conversation in person? Do you want to come to my hotel in about an hour and we can have a chat before heading out for dinner with your friends? I am assuming we are still going?"

I liked it when Lucy was efficient and direct. I tried to be the same in my response. "Yes, to all of that, it sounds perfect, and sorry for interrupting your bath. I will see you soon."

Meeting up in an hour was perfect for me. It gave me time to heat and eat some leftover curry from last night, wash the corn out of my hair and send a quick email report through to the UN about my trip to Oklahoma. It was a bit bureaucratic, but the admin team liked a brief written report every time they sent me an emergency notification.

I also charged both my phones while I was in the shower. The battery on my regular mobile phone did not deal well with rapidly moving across countries and oceans, as constantly switching networks drained it quickly.

I remembered Lucy had said at the taskforce meeting that she was on the board of the Bright eco-electricity company. That seemed a very impressive if slightly unusual role for a university professor. In the shower I wondered idly if there was any chance she could help me jump the queue to get one of the new infinite power phones that had been announced a few months ago and were being released very soon. These phones, powered by a Bright battery, ran continuously for two years without needing to be charged.

———

Once I was ready, as I had plenty of time, I took the Tube to meet Lucy rather than flying a short distance across

London. Once I got off at Hyde Park Corner station it was only a few minutes' walk along Park Lane to Lucy's hotel.

It was now just after 5pm. The streets were busy with people finishing their workdays and going home or heading for a Friday night out in central London. At this time of the year there was still several hours of daylight left, but it was not a particularly warm evening and most people around me had coats or jackets on. I was wearing my long line leather jacket I had on the first time Lucy saw me in civilian clothes, mostly because I thought she liked it. My backpack was in its standard position on my left shoulder.

I was right about the jacket. When Lucy opened her hotel room door to answer my knock the first thing said she said after "Hi" was a rapid, "I was hoping you would wear that jacket tonight. What should I wear, is this ok?" Lucy did a little twirl in the doorway showing off her jeans, black tunic top with sunflowers and yellow sneakers.

I moved towards her, resting my hand casually on her arm as she finished displaying her outfit. Bending my head down I gently kissed Lucy's check and drew her in for a hug.

"You look perfect." Sensing she was a bit nervous about the whole dinner and meeting the friends thing I tried to reassure her. "Dinner will be pretty casual. Many of my friends will come direct from work and the restaurant is not particularly fancy. But the food is good, so I am hope you are hungry, or will be by the time we get there."

"Thank you. Not hungry just yet." Pulling away from my embrace to look at me properly, Lucy asked, "What time do we need to leave here to get to the restaurant? Do we have time for a chat about this afternoon and how we both felt about it? Or is that a conversation for another time?"

"We have a bit of time now," I replied. "It will take

about twenty minutes probably in a cab, so we don't need to leave just yet."

We were still standing in the doorway. When I looked past Lucy and into the hotel room, I noticed it was not just a room but a suite, and we were currently standing in the entrance to a very stylish sitting area with a grey couch facing towards a large window. There was a large work desk to the side of the window that had Lucy's laptop sitting open on it. Through the room to the right was a wide doorway through to the bedroom with sliding doors.

Lucy grabbed my hand and directed me towards the couch. "Sit down, let's talk." I sat.

Rather than waiting for Lucy to explain what was on her mind, I decided to jump right in. "Sorry about today, please don't be too mad at me. I can't really say no when these types of emergencies come up. If we are going to keep seeing each other regularly and just to be very very clear I would really like that because you are wonderful, I am going to be unreliable and what happened today is going to keep happening."

Sitting beside me on the couch, Lucy grabbed my hand and held it tight as she turned to face me. "Do not be sorry, you have nothing to apologise for. And I am not mad." Her words were coming out just a little bit abruptly, which I knew now was a sign Lucy was feeling strong emotions.

"When I said we should talk, I just wanted to get some agreed rules about what to do, what I should do, if you get called off to an emergency. I was concerned today as I was not sure of the right thing to do, but I was not upset with you about leaving. I get that you needed to go. We don't have to resolve it all right now, but we do need to talk about the logistics for our future dates."

"Okay, that's good to know," I responded, relieved

about what Lucy was saying. "As a general rule, I am 100 percent happy with you not waiting around for me to come back. I never know how long something will take. When I get an emergency call, if I have time, I will try and give you an indication if I can before I leave of how long I think it will take. It all depends on what it is. How does that sound?

"Perfect thank you."

Not long later it was time for us to head to Kensington for the birthday dinner. The doorman at the hotel, who was dressed in a top hat and suit with long tails, ushered us into a cab. In the back of the taxi I held Lucy's hand, pointing out more landmarks as we passed by in the London traffic.

When we were nearly at our destination, Lucy twisted slightly in her set and leaned forward slightly towards me. "Do your friends know?" she asked quietly. "About your family origins I mean."

"No. They don't. Except for Tory because he was my friend first, from school. The others all came together as a group in university, so no. Officially I work as an IT security consultant, in sort of an emergency crisis response type role, but I am pretty sure they all think I work for MI6. Pete jokingly calls me Mr Bond all the time, like James Bond. Sorry, I should have told you all that."

"It's fine, just trying to make sure we get our stories straight. I am sure you don't want me spilling any secrets to your friends. Have you thought about telling them though, it might be nice for you to have more of a support network?"

Lucy's question was one that I had asked myself many times over the last few years. "Only about a thousand times," I replied. "But the longer I leave it the weirder it becomes to suddenly say, 'and by the way dot dot dot'."

Conscious that we were in a cab, even though the driver had one earbud in and was carrying on a conversation in Serbian as we drove, I lowered my voice further. "At first, I was unsure of what the public reaction would be, and with Pete being a detective and Josh a journalist I just didn't feel comfortable telling them. Now I feel it's too late. Anyway, my friends will be far more interested in you than in me tonight. It's a long time since I have brought a date to anything like this, so you will be a novelty. They are all very nice people, but you might get lots of questions."

"We're here," I said as the taxi slowed in front of a row of brightly lit shopfronts that lined the road. I paid the driver, thanking him in Serbian just because I could, and then leapt out, reaching back in to offer Lucy a hand. Once I had her right hand clasped firmly in my left one, we walked through the door and into the restaurant. I was very pleased to have Lucy by my side tonight.

The restaurant was a casual and cozy Italian place on the ground floor of a Victorian era building. It was one big open space, the internal walls long since removed, with exposed iron pillars dotted across the floor space. In the back left corner, there was a large wood fired pizza oven which radiated heat across the space and also filled the room with a delightful aroma.

Lucy had paused at the front of the restaurant, unsure where to go. I raised our joined hands and pointed towards a long table to our right. "Over there, that's Dev and Emma, Dylan, Tory and Pete. Are you ready?"

We weaved through the crush of tables, still hand in hand. It was slightly difficult to navigate through the room that way, but I didn't want to let Lucy go.

"Hi, hello everyone." I stopped with Lucy beside me in front of a couple of empty seats at the table. Everyone turned and smiled up at us with a chorus of hellos and good evenings.

"Everyone, this is Lucy. Lucy is an American, she is a physicist, she doesn't know anything about our kind of football, and I think she is absolutely lovely." Lucy giggled slightly beside me, blushing slightly at my words.

Pointing at everyone in turn I went around the table. "This is Pete, Tory, Dylan, Dev the birthday boy and Emma, and we are still waiting on Josh."

Looking around at everyone in turn Lucy said, "Hi, it's nice to meet you all and happy birthday Dev, thanks for letting me join in the celebrations. Curtis has told me mostly nothing about you all, so I am looking forward to getting to know you tonight."

The waiter arrived with menus, and then Josh arrived with a flurry of apologies for being late even though he wasn't actually late, just last to arrive, and we all settled into the evening.

Josh had taken the empty seat to Lucy's right, and that gave him the prime position to start peppering her with questions once we had all placed our food orders. "So, Lucy, give us all your details," Josh probed. "I'm a journalist so I am required by law to ask lots of questions, starting with how you ended up with Curtis when there must be hundreds of millions of American men closer to home for you?"

Lucy seemed relaxed and comfortable as she answered. "I'm a scientist, so I am also required to ask lots of questions and do lots of research, so I understand where you are coming from Josh."

"Curtis and I met at a work conference a few weeks

ago," Lucy explained. "We bonded over the terrible food at the event and got talking. I live in New York, but I come to the UK regularly, as I am part of a research group that has some members here, so I am often on this side of the pond. I came down to London last night after a few days in Oxford at a symposium, and Curtis has been showing me all the tourist sights today."

Our garlic bread arrived but that didn't slow down Josh's playful questioning. "So you're a physicist? Tell us what sort of physics and whether you have a white lab coat?"

Lucy paused slightly before answering this one, I assumed thinking about how best to succinctly answer without providing an in-depth run down of her complex back story. She seemed a little reserved about talking about herself and her achievements. Distracting myself from taking more than my fair share of the garlic bread, I reached over and put my hand on Lucy's thigh under the table to provide reassurance. She turned slightly towards me with a quick smile in response.

Focusing again on Josh, Lucy continued, "I am a physicist and an engineer, and yes, I have a white lab coat but don't wear it much. I am on staff at Endeavour University in New York, and that's mostly supervision of grad students, and I am also a professor at Logan Technology Institute in Boston, where I mostly do research work. That work is more practically based so I am often in a lab, but I tend just to wear regular clothes without a lab coat. Sorry to disappoint."

Josh smiled. "No, I'm sorry I made the conversation all about your clothing choices. That sounds all pretty cool. The Logan Technology physics department must be an interesting place to work. That's where the clean energy breakthroughs were made a few years back wasn't it? You know the eco-electricity inventions made by that Professor Smith guy that weirdly no one would tell us who he was? I always thought that was odd that someone would develop amazing new technology and then try and keep their identity secret." Josh paused for a moment. "Hey, maybe you know who he is?"

My hand was still resting on Lucy's thigh so I could feel the moment her entire body tensed up in response to Josh's comments. She swallowed hard and seemed lost for words. Something he said had made her very uncomfortable.

I jumped back into the conversation to deflect away from Josh's line of questioning. As much as I was curious about what had made Lucy tense up, if she did not want to tell Josh, or me, then I was very happy to force a change of subject. "So, Josh, how is your work going? I read that piece you wrote on the crime gangs in South London, that was very interesting. Were you happy with where it landed?"

The release of tension in Lucy confirmed I had made the right decision. Josh looked at me with a slightly confused expression but then launched into a long discussion with me about his article, and his plans for a follow up piece next month. Emma leaned forward across the table to ask Lucy about her favourite part of the sight-seeing in London had been so far.

Although the conversation moved on, Lucy's reaction to Josh's question stayed with me. I wondered why she had been triggered by Josh discussing the eco-electricity research when, as I understood it, she was involved in the company that was marketing this invention.

We finished up at the restaurant just before 10pm, as no-one wanted a late night. Over dessert, I had seen Lucy stifling a yawn while talking to Tory. When we arrived at back at Lucy's hotel, I walked with her back to her room but then paused outside the door. I could tell Lucy was exhausted from the physical and emotional intensity of the day.

"Thanks for a lovely evening and a wonderful day Dr Lucy," I said, trying to keep my voice warm and tender. "I really enjoyed it, and I am looking forward to whatever we end up doing tomorrow. You seem very tired, so I am going to kiss you good night, and leave you to get some sleep. Call me when you wake up."

Chapter 14
Lucy

The first call I made when I woke up was to room service, to order a latte to be brought up to the room. My second call was to Cyran, to let him know I was awake. "Good morning, Dr Lucy." Cyran sounded full of energy as he answered his phone. "How are you this morning?"

"I am okay thank you, but my legs and feet are a bit sore. All the walking from yesterday has obviously caught up with me, so I need a relatively quiet start to the day and not so much physical activity I think."

"How about we do something really low key then?" Cyran asked. "Would you like to come and see my place, and we could go around the corner to my favourite cafe for brunch? Their coffee is very good. No rush, whenever you get here."

That sounded perfect. "Great idea, text me your address please and I will let you know when I am on my way. I am just having a coffee sent up, and then I will get ready and come over."

Taking Cyran at his word that there was no rush to get

to his place, I progressed my morning routine slowly. I was a little embarrassed about my reaction to Josh's questions last night and concerned about what Cyran would think. The slow start and the cab ride over to Cyran's gave me some time to think through how best to talk to him about the parts of my life story I had not yet shared.

Cyran's apartment was lovely. The outside was a gorgeous art deco building in warm red brick, and the inside a well-renovated modern space that still retained the original character of the building.

"If the brunch can wait a few minutes, can we talk about something before we go and eat?" I asked as Cyran finished giving me a quick tour of his flat. "I want to clear something up about what happened last night, and I am nervous about it, so I want to get it over."

"Of course, but only if you are okay to talk about. Let's sit in the living room for a bit. The sofa is the best place for deep and meaningful conversations."

Cyran grabbed my hand and led me through to the lounge, where there was a well-loved comfy looking brown couch facing a very large television. We sat down next to each other with hands still touching. I turned my body inwards to face Cyran, but hung my head low, looking at our hands rather than Cyran's face.

Deep breath in and out. "So, I am sorry that I froze up last night when Josh started asking me about the invention of eco-electricity and whether I knew Professor Smith the mystery inventor. It is a question I have been asked many times before, and I do have a standard answer I generally use, but last night I did not know what to say."

I paused and looked up at Cyran, who smiled and nodded at me. "Don't be sorry, I was just worried about Josh having upset you."

Dropping my gaze to stare intently at Cyran's fingers, I continued. "You know how I told you on our first date that I had started college at Logan Institute of Technology at twelve years old? Well, I was still studying at Logan a few years later when the eco-electricity technology was invented. By me, the technology was invented by me. I struggled to answer Josh's question because he was actually asking me about myself, and I did not want to lie to you and your friends."

"Oh, okay. That's very cool." I could practically hear Cyran's mind processing this. "That's amazing, and it all makes more sense now." He dropped my hand and leaned forward to wrap both his arms around me, pulling my body towards me so we were pressed tightly together in a close hug for a few glorious moments.

Releasing us from the hug, Cyran restarted the conversation. "Can I ask why you kept it all a secret though? You must have missed out on a lot of recognition and awards by hiding your success."

Cyran was right, but I could explain to him why I was keeping my invention secret. "At the time I invented eco-electricity I was just fifteen years old. My parents were very worried about the impact that negative media and public responses would have on me, and so they decided to shelter me from all the publicity. The university came up with the Professor Smith idea to give credit to someone who didn't exist."

"Yes, I have missed out on recognition," I continued, "but I also got to finish growing up out of the spotlight. I am sure you can understand that, *Curtis*." I used that name deliberately.

"Good point, yes. My parents and the UK Government did sort of the same for me."

"At the NASA taskforce meeting, I introduced myself as being on the board of the Bright Eco-electricity company. This is true, I am on the board, but I also founded the company when I was eighteen. While I sold a chunk of the ownership of the company early on, I am very involved with company still and it is something very important to me."

"Because of hiding that part of my history, I am not very comfortable talking to people about the work that I do, my achievements and the science I love so much. After I sold part of my company, I started to also worry about people only wanting to be friends with me because I was now ridiculously wealthy. My friends Kane and Ellie both know, but that's about it outside the family and the people I directly work with. I am sorry I didn't tell you earlier, I just needed to feel comfortable first that you liked the real me first."

"Very much," Cyran murmured reassuringly.

"This doesn't mean, though, that I will suddenly become comfortable telling other people."

"Oh yes, I understand that," Cyran said. "I feel the same way about telling people my history. The Prime Minister knows my secret identity but not the people I go to the pub with. But I am also not keen on them possibly looking at me differently."

Cyran was thoughtful as he continued, "I also under-stand about hiding, and how hard that can be sometimes. I know it is not the same but found it really hard to adjust to acting like a normal kid when I was first here on Earth and throughout my teenage years."

"Being able to fly and being fast and strong was normal for me on my home planet. As a teenager, I was constantly being told my parents and my handlers in the Government to suppress my normal behaviours so that I could fit in and assimilate. 'Don't do that in public. Don't fly, don't run fast' etc."

Wow that was intense. I could feel myself tearing up, my empathy for teenage Cyran making me emotional. "I am sorry you had to go through all that when you were younger," I said gently. "Hiding is hard." Cyran nodded and held my hand.

"So, just to pick up on something you said in amongst all that, as well as being incredibly smart and very sexy, you are also, to use your words, ridiculously wealthy?" Cyran asked.

"Umm, yes."

Cyran paused before he responded. "Honestly, I am not sure what to say here without it coming out weird. 'That's great, glad you are very rich sounds a bit off."

I laughed. "Yes, it definitely has benefits, but it's another secret I need to keep from people." I stood up, suddenly in need of more coffee and a break from the intensity of this conversation. "Come on, let's go get some food now if we have finished with the big reveals."

"Great, I am starving. Just give be a couple of minutes." Cyran dashed off to the bathroom to put his contact lenses in, and returned with blue eyes instead of gold, ready to go out in public.

The cafe where we went for brunch was a fabulous little family-run place, just around the corner from Cyran's flat as he had promised. The design theme was exposed brick, pendant light globes and minimalist design. The staff knew Cyran by name and seemed intrigued by the fact that he had someone with him this morning. I noticed the young barista whispering to an older lady who seemed like the owner as they glanced in our direction.

As we waited for coffee and full English breakfasts, our conversation was deliberately light. Cyran tried to explain the league structure of English football to me, and I sat back and let him talk, enjoying the sound of his voice, without specifically caring about what he was saying or taking much of what he was saying in. The only thing that registered was that his team had done well last season.

I mentioned that my niece played junior soccer, and how Kane's Community Mart funded community junior sports programs. I then realised I could now explain to Cyran about how Kane and I had founded the Kane's Community Mart business. Cyran was fascinated with our model of using the profits of the supermarket to support the local communities. As we discussed it, I was reminded that Cyran, like Kane, spent most of his time also helping vulnerable people and communities, albeit in a different way. Cyran and Kane would probably get on quite well with their shared passion for helping others.

Thinking about my best friend meeting the new man, I suggested to Cyran that we should get together with Kane sometime for dinner in New York.

"Do we double date? Does Kane have a significant other?" Cyran asked.

"No, not at the moment. His last boyfriend was a bit of a loser. Kane was very hurt when he found out Duncan was cheating on him."

Cyran swore quietly.

"Kane was working long hours at the time, flying all over the country to get the new stores in Iowa and Mississippi set up, but that's not an excuse for what Duncan did."

"Agreed."

When our breakfasts arrived, it was a shock. Cyran had ordered us both full English breakfasts, with double toast, so I was presented with a large plate filled with sausages, thick English style bacon, baked beans, two fried eggs, mushrooms, tomatoes and a mountain of toast. I was hungry and it looked delicious, but there was no way I was going to eat all that food.

"I hope you are going to help with this?" I asked Cyran, waving my hands across my plate with its giant pile of breakfast.

"Yep, of course. I hope you don't mind. It's going to be a good perk of having a girlfriend that you can help me order more food than is socially acceptable for me to eat."

"So that's the way we formalise our relationship? Over shared bacon?" I asked slightly bemused as this is the first time Cyran or I had put a label on it.

"Um, yes? How do you feel about making it official? I would love to be your boyfriend if you think that it could work between us even though we are based on different sides of the Atlantic."

I didn't need time to think about what Cyran was asking, as I knew that I wanted to formalise our relationship. "I would like that too, very much," I confirmed. "I think we have a secret advantage in the long-distance relationship stakes. Although explaining this to our friends and family is going to get a bit complicated."

"Very complicated indeed," Cyran sighed. "Your family is probably going to hate me as I am going to be a deadbeat boyfriend sometimes and not show up to a bunch of things."

"They won't hate you. And where my family are concerned it won't matter, because I like you and they will just have to respect that," I reassured him. "We will just need a cover story for you disappearing. Hopefully it will be like with your friends where they think you are a spy." My boyfriend the spy would be much easier to explain that my boyfriend the alien superhero.

Brunch was a slow and very relaxed meal after that. Cyran ate his breakfast and most of mine, and we went back for a second round of coffees. Last night during the trip back to my hotel Cyran and I had vaguely discussed a few ideas for things to do today, but I had been too tired to really commit to anything last night. His suggestions had ranged from visiting some more touristy places, such as the Tower of London, or some more local authentic experiences like visiting a weekend street market.

In the end we did none of those things. When we walked back to Cyran's flat from the cafe it was already early afternoon. A few hours had passed comfortably while we were chatting and then eating brunch. I was relieved that we had been able to be so honest with each other, but I was feeling a lot of emotional as well as physical fatigue.

I had an early morning flight home Sunday morning, so we decided to take the rest of the day very slowly. We spent a few hours taking a slow walk together along the riverbank and had takeaway pizza for dinner snuggled up on the couch together while Cyran watched a football match on TV. It was heavenly.

Chapter 15
Cyran

The rest of the month of June went by very quickly after Lucy left London. Now that we had put our relationship on a more formal basis, I was spending most of my free evenings with Lucy. It was even possible for me to do something in the evening in London and then head to the US for a whole second evening once Lucy was finished work for the day.

We were spending most of our time at Lucy's place in New York. On the day of our Central Park date a few weeks ago, I had wondered whether Lucy was embarrassed by her apartment. It turned out she was just reticent to show me her amazing home while she was still keeping secrets about her history and financial situation.

The house had good access for me to fly in undetected. When it was dark I felt very comfortable coming and going from the back terrace on the second level. When it was light, I was more cautious, and if it seemed there were neighbours around in their gardens I always landed in the alleyway behind the bank on the nearby cross street and then made my way around the corner to avoid being spotted.

Only once in late June did I get distracted from spending time with Lucy by an emergency, and that was me not arriving on a Tuesday night for a planned lazy evening of wine and takeout. It was the start of summer holidays in the northern hemisphere and there were lots of accidents and emergencies caused by winter in the southern hemisphere, but thankfully there was nothing major that kept me away from home for days at a time.

Lucy had told her parents about me, all the non-classified bits anyway. We had made plans for me to officially come to the US for the Fourth of July weekend, so I could meet everyone at the big family dinner Lucy's parents were hosting. I was going to fly in on the Thursday and stay in New York through the long weekend. A dinner with Kane was planned as well while I was in town, so I could meet him and apparently get the 'if you hurt my best friend, I will kill you' talk out of the way.

I was putting off making plans for Lucy to meet my parents, not quite ready to deal with confessing to my parents that I had an American girlfriend. My parents should definitely like Lucy as a person, but I was worried how they would react to me having so quickly revealed my secret identity to Lucy and that they would want me to officially tell the UK Government about our relationship. I felt like our relationship was no-one's business but ours.

The last weekend in June, I was at Lucy's house on the Saturday morning, having just arrived so we could go out to breakfast together. Lucy was in the bathroom, still getting ready, as apparently she had been distracted in the shower with a good idea and had needed to write her thoughts down. She was preparing for a busy week ahead in Washington working with the scientists on the taskforce, so she no doubt had lots of things on her mind.

I was in no hurry for breakfast, particularly as I had already had an early breakfast catchup a couple of hours ago with Tory, Pete and Josh before they headed off on a day's hike. It had been one of our traditions since uni days, a couple times a year in good weather having a giant fry up for breakfast followed a day meandering through the English countryside. These days I only went to the breakfast, using needing to be on call for my IT job as my excuse.

Making myself comfortable on the giant sectional sofa in the casual living area off Lucy's kitchen, I flicked the TV on to pass the time, flicking channels until I found coverage of the first-round matches at Wimbledon.

Lucy came rushing down the stairs about 10 minutes later and kissed me hello. "Apologies, sorry to keep you waiting so long."

"No need to be sorry, there's no rush," I reassured her. "I am enjoying watching the tennis. It is happening only a few miles from my home, which is a bit weird having just flown across the Atlantic away from London."

"Pretty sure most things you do are a bit weird." Lucy's retort was blunt but true, and I said as much.

My personal phone rang just as we were ready to leave the house. It wasn't a work call, so I was very tempted to let it go to voicemail. When I did pull the phone out of my jeans pocket, the screen showed me it was Tory calling. It was odd that he was calling me now, as he should be off hiking somewhere in the great outdoors with Pete and Josh.

"Hello, aren't you supposed to be out hiking?" I asked by way of greeting.

Tory's voice was shaking as he responded. "Yes, but Josh is hurt. He's bad. He fell. The ambulance won't be here for an hour, and oh god, Pete reckons he might, ... that he might not have that long. He hit his head, and it looks like he has a serious head injury."

"Damn." That was the only word my brain could supply at that point.

"I was hoping, you know, you could organise to help," Tory asked. "Josh really needs to get to a hospital quickly."

I snapped into problem solving mode. "Of course, I will be there in a couple of minutes. Where are you exactly? Can you send me your location? When we hang up, I need you to do three things. Make sure Josh has his ID in his pocket, send your exact location to my phone, and do a search on your phone to find the nearest major hospital to where you are. It will be quicker and easier for me if I know where to go."

Lucy was standing across the room looking concerned as she had heard my side of the conversation. "That was Tory," I explained once I hung up. "Josh has had a bad fall, and they are an hour away from an ambulance getting there. I am going to take him to hospital."

"Off you go, don't waste time talking to me," Lucy responded. "Fly safe and keep me up to date as much as you can."

As I was changing into my flight suit upstairs, my phone binged with a text message notification. It showed my friends' location in the Wych Forest about 40 miles south of London. Easy, I could be there in less than 90 seconds if I pushed my flying speed to the limit.

The location icon Tory had sent to my phone showed they were out in in the open countryside, and as I got closer, I could see three figures at the base of a rocky granite outcrop that stood about five metres high. One of them was Tory, waving frantically to get my attention.

Josh was lying on his side in the recovery position at the bottom of the rocky outcrop, with Pete at this side. It didn't take much to imagine Josh rushing up to the top of the rocks to see the view, or check their location, or just for fun. Josh then falling to the ground I did not want to imagine. I was very accustomed to seeing people in distress, but they were usually strangers. It felt very different having to rescue my own friends and when I saw Josh on the ground I struggled to get my own emotions of fear and panic under control.

I landed a little way away from the group so that the air rush of my coming in at high speed did not disturb Josh and then hurried across the grass towards my friends. Tory was looking at me cautiously, clearly unsure exactly what to say and whether to acknowledge me as his friend.

"Hello," I called out as I got closer. "Looks like you need some help."

Pete was kneeling beside Josh's unconscious form on the ground, and he looked up at the sound of my voice. "Oh my God," he said in a shocked tone and then quickly switched to his more matter-of-fact police officer voice. "Thank goodness you are here. Thank you for coming. This man is badly injured and needs a hospital immediately. Can you take him to the Regent Hospital in Hayworth? It's probably the closest emergency room."

The words sounded oddly formal coming from my friend of nearly 10 years. Pete obviously hadn't immediately recognised me, which was a good thing, as right now the focus needed to be getting Josh to a hospital, not discussing my secret identity.

"Of course." I matched Pete's formally with some of my

own. "Please give me a very quick overview of what happened and any treatment so far that I can relay that to the hospital staff."

Looking at his watch, Pete replied, "His name is Joshua Preston. Age 32. Approximately 9 minutes ago he felt from a height of roughly eight metres. Obvious compound fracture to the left leg, but also likely head injury. He has been unconscious since the fall. No response to stimulus."

"Right. I will take him. Are you both alright, or are you also injured?"

"We're fine. Just go. Look after Josh." This was Tory who had been standing to one side.

"Come on, Pete, we need to stand back." He gently pulled Pete up to standing and walked them both back out of my way.

I gently picked Josh up, keeping him still on his side in the recovery position and protecting his head and neck from any movement. I raised my head upwards and lifted off for a vertical take-off, keeping my speed low to protect Josh.

A few minutes later, for it was a much slower trip with a seriously injured man in my arms, I landed in the ambulance bay at the nearby hospital. Four ambulances were lined up in the bay, and there was a set of double sliding doors off to one side.

I was about halfway to the doors when they burst open, and a nurse came out to meet me. She was obviously tired, perhaps well into her shift, but she greeted me with a small smile. "Come in this way," she called. "Bring them straight through." Inside the doorway there was a stretcher waiting and the nurse gestured for me to place

Josh onto it. "On his back please if you can manage roll him over."

The two other staff members who were standing in the hallway started working on Josh immediately, examining and taking his vitals. "Who do we have here?" one of them asked me.

"His name is Joshua Preston according to his friends." Very professionally, as officially I didn't know this man, I went on to explain the situation by repeating Pete's words about what had happened to Josh and described the first aid he had been given.

"That's great, we will take it from here. And thank you, this man is very lucky you were able to get him to the hospital so quickly."

Walking out of the emergency department I was at a bit of a loss. I couldn't stay, because then I would have to admit that Josh was a friend of mine, but it felt wrong leaving him alone.

It seemed I had been spotted arriving on my way in. A small crowd had now gathered in the ambulance bay, a couple of whom were shouting my name. I hated fan girls and thought it so inappropriate that they were stalking me at a hospital when a man was fighting for his life. I turned towards the crowd and just gave them a "Hello everyone" before making my way out of the ambulance bay and launching myself into the open sky.

Wanting to check my phone for any messages from Tory, I landed again in a field not far out of the town. A bunch of sheep wandered up towards me to see what was going on and so I stood in the field, surrounded by sheep, and made a call to Tory.

"Thank goodness, how did it go, is he alright?" Tory got straight to the point when he answered his phone.

"It went fine. No change in his vitals or status. I dropped him at the hospital and told the staff everything and then left him there." I sighed. "It felt awful to have to do that, Tory."

Tory sounded sympathetic. "I imagine it did, but you probably saved Josh's life. Pete and I are on our way back to the car. We should be there in about fifteen minutes and then will head to the hospital. Perhaps you could meet us at the car? It's at the north carpark. Maybe with some coffee and food if you can manage that? We are both cold and in a bit of shock, I think. Oh, and I have rung Josh's parents, they are on the way down to the hospital from London as well."

As I processed all that, Tory continued, "And, mate, I need to tell Pete what is going on. He is no doubt very confused, particularly as he can hear my half of this conversation. You okay if I out you?" Of course, Tory hadn't really given me any choice in this, if he had taken my call with Pete in earshot.

"Yep, that's fine," I replied. "I should have done it a long time ago. See you in a bit at your car."

"Thanks, see you soon."

With the inquisitive sheep still keeping me company in the field, I sent a text to Lucy.

> Not good news at all, Josh is badly hurt, he fell off a rock during the hiking trip. I have just airlifted him to hospital and need to go back and help Tory and Pete. Raincheck on breakfast?

Lucy's response came in pretty much instantly. She must have had her phone in her hand.

DR LUCY

Of course. Glad you got him to the hospital
so quick. Keep me posted.

On the way into the hospital, I had noticed a large chain
coffee place in town, and it was one I regularly visited at
home in London. I opened their app on my phone and
placed an order for three large coffees, plus some toasted
sandwiches and bagels. Then I flew back into town, found a
secluded spot to change into my civilian clothes, and pulled
a pair of sunglasses out of my backpack so I didn't need to
worry about hiding the colour of my eyes. I felt stupid
wearing sunglasses inside, but I did it on occasions like this
when trying to avoid the hassle of putting my contact lenses
in and out quickly.

The coffee gods were obviously smiling on me, as a staff
member called out "Order for Curtis" about two minutes
after I walked through the door of the cafe. Another clothes
change later, because I did not want to get caught flying
wearing regular clothes, I headed to the sky again. I soon
realised that it was quite hard to fly while carrying three
coffees on a tray. I have many abilities, but it turns out that
is not one of them.

When Pete and Tory approached the carpark area,
what was left of the coffees was balancing on the roof of
Tory's car, and I was casually resting against the front of the
vehicle. Both men seemed exhausted. Pete looked intently
at me as they came closer. "So, mate, I hear there is something you have been meaning to tell us for a while now," he
said, grinning. "That's pretty cool, but you could have
found a better way to break it to us than getting Josh to
jump off a cliff."

With that, I figured our friendship was going to be okay.

Chapter 16
Lucy

The week after Josh's accident, Cyran had stayed in London most of the time, as he wanted to be close by if there was anything he could do to help Josh and his parents.

Josh was awake, and Cyran told me mid-week that after multiple scans the doctors were confident that there was not likely to be any long-term brain trauma. Josh had been moved to a major hospital in central London for surgery on his leg and was going to be in hospital for a while yet. Cyran also told me that he had had a long talk with Pete and Tory on Sunday night, debriefing the accident and discussing Cyran's backstory.

I had spent Monday through Wednesday in Washington working on the taskforce project. We had worked late on Wednesday evening to avoid coming back in on Thursday, with the aim of giving everyone a chance to head home before the Fourth of July holiday on Friday.

By lunchtime on Thursday I was home from Washington, having endured two very busy airports crammed with people who like me were keen to get home. When I opened my front door, the house smelled crisp and clean, as my cleaning service had been in the day before. Conscious of Cyran's appetite, I had also done a large online grocery shop last night that would be delivered later today, ordering a range of healthy foods we could eat together and high calorie snacks if he needed them.

Cyran planned to fly in on Thursday evening to spend the weekend with me, but I had told my parents that my new boyfriend Curtis was arriving on Friday morning from London. The little white lie was just one of many we were going tell across the weekend about Cyran, but this one was very selfish as I wanted some alone time with him without any chance of my parents suddenly deciding to visit or contacting me.

About 5pm, I heard a thump on the back terrace and looked up from where I was pretending to be reading emails at the kitchen table to see Cyran standing on the deck with a regular four wheeled suitcase beside him. It was a weird look. Carrying rather than wheeling the suitcase he came through into the house, and putting the case down, he gave me a huge hug.

"I have missed you Dr Lucy, it has been five whole days since I last saw you."

I loved it when he called me that stupid nickname. "I missed you too."

Cyran got changed and unpacked a few things into the space I had cleared for him in my walk-in closet while I ordered us some dinner.

After a relaxed meal it was not long before we headed upstairs. It had been a slow burn, but we were both now very ready for the next step in our relationship. We walked along the corridor to the master bedroom hand in hand, and then in the doorway Cyran leaned down to scoop me up and to carry me across the threshold into my own bedroom. As we entered the room, with me giggling in his arms, he turned and firmly pushed the bedroom door shut behind us, shutting off our little haven of togetherness from the outside world.

The following morning, I woke to the light streaming through the slats of the window blinds.

I was alone, but that was not surprising. I didn't expect Cyran to be still in bed nearly eight hours later. I just hoped he was somewhere in the house rather than somewhere in Europe or Antarctica.

Coming out of the bathroom a few minutes later, I found Cyran sitting on the side of the bed, holding two mugs. He must have heard me get up. He was wearing boxer shorts and a t-shirt, and his hair was down, flowing around his face. For a brief moment the amazingly handsome colour of his eyes caught me off guard. I was still not used to spending large amounts of time with him without contact lenses hiding his alien look.

"Good morning, Dr Lucy," he said with a smile, handing me the hot drink in his left hand. "Sorry, this is tea. I was sure you would want coffee, but I cannot figure out how to drive your fancy coffee machine. Did you sleep well?

"Very well, thank you." Leaning in to give him a kiss, I asked, "What about you, did you sleep?"

"A few hours, which is pretty good for me. I have been here all night though, doing some computer stuff and watching some TV. I love the size of your house. I can hang out in the living spaces downstairs and not worry about waking you up. At my place me clattering around in the kitchen would wake you up."

"Umm that's good." I was listening but focused on drinking my tea.

"Only drama was that I didn't have the WIFI password for working on my laptop. I'll get it off you sometime today."

Such domestic bliss, discussing WIFI at 7am.

We had made no plans for the day and were completely free until we were due to be at my parents for family dinner at 6pm. The plan was that we would eat early and then as it got dark, walk up the road to find a high spot to watch the fireworks over the city.

Today it was my turn to play tour guide for Cyran, showing him some of my favourite parts of the city. We started off walking, knowing that it would get too hot later and we would need to take to the subway or a cab. Walking through to Central Park, we headed down through the park until we hit the American Museum of Natural History. It was closed today for the holiday, so we then took the subway south to Times Square, where I bought Cyran the classic I heart NYC t-shirt, and he promised to never wear it.

I was blissfully happy as we walked through the hot crowded streets hand in hand, discussing landmarks and the city's history. Cyran stayed with me all day, with no emergency call outs interrupting our time together.

I had organised a car to come just after 5pm to take us out to Queens. On the way I gave Cyran more of a run down on my family's backstory. It was not yet something we had yet discussed, other than me telling him about my family moving to Boston with me for college.

I explained how my parents are both immigrants and I grew up speaking both Spanish and English at home. I also told Cyran that I felt guilty for uprooting my parents out of their community in the move to Boston and but how well they had adjusted coming back to New York. "They took the opportunity to retire soon after we all moved back, and now they are involved in heaps of community activities, as well as spending lots of time helping with my sister and brothers' kids."

The traffic out of the city was more terrible than I had expected, and it was well past 6pm when we arrived at my parent's home. As we pulled up Cyran turned towards me. He lowered his voice to a conspiratorial whisper and said, "Anything I need to know before we go in? Topics to avoid, crazy people to not talk to?"

With a laugh I replied, "No to both. I mean it will probably be a bit intense, and they will bombard us both with light-hearted questions, but I am sure they will like you. I am just a bit nervous though, I don't often bring boys home to meet the family."

My parents had obviously seen the car stop on the street, as they were now standing on the front porch looking over towards the car. Dad had his left hand resting on Mom's shoulder, a warm familiar gesture.

"Game face on. Let's do this." I turned to Cyran, but he had leapt out of the car and was tipping the driver. He raced around to open my door for me. Taking my hand, we walked together up the path to meet the parents. Bounding up the three steps to the porch, Cyran smiled as he held his hand out to my father.

"Hello Mr and Mrs Cortez, lovely to meet you. I'm

Curtis Harrington." With his British accent he sounded charming.

My dad shook Cyran's hand, at the same time shaking his head at formality. "No need to be that fancy, I'm Pedro and this is my wife Val. Welcome to our home."

Mom leaned forward to hug me, and then Cyran. "You are most definitely very welcome." Pulling back, she turned to face us both. "Come on inside you two. Lucia hasn't told us anything about you, so we have lots to discuss. Is that accent English?"

"Yes, I'm from London, but the organisation I work for is headquartered in New York, so I spend a lot of time here in the States." Cyran didn't like having to lie, and this was all true, I suppose, leaving out some key details.

Walking in the front door, I shepherded Cyran down the hall past a series of closed doors and through to the large open plan kitchen and living room at the back of the house. The house was 1950s vintage, with the original rooms at the front now used as a study and a guest room, and heart of the house being the open plan extension with a back wall of sliding glass doors that opened onto the deck and the grassed yard beyond.

This space was full of people, including a bunch of children of various ages. My sister Gabriela was directing the food prep, a group of my brothers and my brother-in-law were discussing hockey, and Timothy, aged five, was racing around brandishing a pirate sword. It was loud and a bit crazy, but I always enjoyed coming home.

As we walked in, Mom announced, "Look who's here!" The noise suddenly stopped as all the adults turned towards us.

"Hi everyone," I said. "This is my boyfriend, Curtis."

And then of course everyone started speaking at once,

issuing hellos, and my brothers came forward to shake Cyran's hand. From the kitchen I heard Gabriela discussing loudly in Spanish how this Curtis was so very attractive.

Beside me Cyran laughed and then raised his voice to talk over the crowd. "Hi everyone, it's nice to meet you all." And then switching to flawless Spanish he said, "Thanks for inviting me to join family dinner. I'm looking forward to getting to know the important people in Lucy's life. And I should probably mention I speak Spanish."

Lots of laughter greeted this statement. "He's going to fit in well here," said my dad.

After a few more introductions, it wasn't long before it felt safe to leave Cyran alone in the living room with the rest of the men to bond, beer in hand. I made my way into the kitchen. Mom just squeezed my hand and said quietly, "He seems lovely dear," and put me to work grating cheese.

When the food was ready, and all the adults had sat down to dinner around the large kitchen table, everyone suddenly had questions for Cyran and me. The kids had all eaten first and were now curled up like a bunch of puppies on the large sectional sofa in the living room watching an animated movie.

"So, Curtis, tell us about yourself." Marco, my oldest brother, started the interrogation/friendly questioning. "Lucy has given us no detail at all."

Cyran took a breath. I could almost hear his brain switching gears to make sure the right version of his life story was the one he provided to my family. "As you can probably tell from my accent, I am British. I grew up in London and now live both in London and New York, depending on my work situation. I work as a security consultant for a New York based organisation, and my work takes me all over the world, sometimes on an emergency basis, so I travel a lot."

"And where did you guys meet?" asked Gabriela.

We had rehearsed this one, so I was confident to answer it. "Curtis and I met at a conference in Washington a few months ago. A few days later he came to campus and asked me out." All true.

"And it was love at first scientific presentation?" Gabriela asked teasingly. "Or did your eyes meet across the lecture theatre?" Arghh, sisters, I thought. I decided just to ignore the question.

Cyran was smiling though, and he didn't seem too embarrassed as he told Gabriela that he had first chatted me up at the lunch break, casually pointing out that, "It was more love at first sandwich."

"Well, that can't be true," Gabriela huffed. "Lucy doesn't eat sandwiches. We all know that." She looked perplexed when Cyran and I both started laughing. "Okay, I imagine there is a story there. Let's have all the details."

"We actually bonded over my hatred of sandwiches," I explained. "I could not face the food provided at the meeting, which was sandwiches and orange juice, and when Curtis noticed I was not eating anything he came over to check if I was alright. He then made a special trip out of the building to get me something decent to eat, which was very lovely of him."

There was a collective "Awwwww" around the table.

"That's so sweet, Lucia," Mom gushed. "Curtis sounds like a keeper."

"He's right here Mom, but yes I think so too." Cyran reached under the table to touch my leg, telling me wordlessly that he agreed with my mother as well.

Thankfully the focus then shifted off our new relationship and on to other topics.

Chapter 17
Cyran

D inner with the Cortez family last night had gone really well. Lucy's family had all been very welcoming, and it had been a novel experience for me to be immersed in a family that was so loud and openly loving. My parents were loving, but in a more restrained way, and they were certainly not loud.

Tonight was our scheduled dinner with Lucy's friend Kane. Lucy had decided to host Kane at her place, rather than us going to a restaurant, telling me that she would be most comfortable with the meeting of her two favourite people being somewhere private. I wondered if that meant she was nervous about us getting along well. I was sure Kane knew Lucy much better than I did as they had been friends for nearly a decade now.

Lucy had planned to get food delivered from a local restaurant, but I offered to cook instead, as I had the time and access to Lucy's magnificent kitchen. About half my London flat could have fitted in the space taken up by her kitchen and butler's pantry. After discussions with Lucy about any dietary requirements Kane may have I settled on moussaka, with a Greek salad and fresh bread.

We filled our day Saturday by going out to breakfast and then doing a great deal of shopping. Our first stop was at a local homewares store for a baking dish and other utensils I needed to cook with and then we did a huge grocery shop. Lucy's pantry was very empty. Even though she had stocked up with food for my visit, she didn't cook, and I had to buy basics like herbs and flour as well as the specific ingredients for our meal.

As we walked to the big chain grocery store a few blocks from Lucy's house, I queried with Lucy whether we should be shopping at a Kane's Community Market, particularly given the CEO of that business was coming dinner tonight. "There are no Kane's in the Upper West Side," Lucy explained. "Not really our target demographic. We set up in places where we can provide the best support to disadvantaged communities. Of course, there are vulnerable people in all parts of the city though."

"That makes sense," I agreed.

"I am sure today Kane will forgive us, particularly as it is so hot and I don't want to be trekking all over the city."

I had not grocery shopped in America before and it was interesting doing a comparison between what was available in here and in my local supermarket in Chelsea. The store was cool and relatively quiet. It seemed that many of the locals were not in the city for the weekend or were at least spending their Saturdays somewhere other than the grocery store.

I was in the kitchen finalising the salad when Kane arrived, and I held back slightly to let Lucy greet him at the door and bring him through the house, conscious that they probably wanted a moment of time together. I could have listened in to their conversation if I had wanted to but restrained myself from doing so. Finishing chopping the tomato, I rinsed my hands in the kitchen sink, not wanting to ruin my first impression by shaking hands with tomato juice all over me.

Lucy said that the dinner tonight would be a very casual both in vibe and in dress standards, so I had taken my lead from her and was just wearing jeans and a short sleeve button down shirt.

A moment later the two of them came through from the hallway into the kitchen. Kane was dressed in skinny black jeans and a tight fit purple and white checked button down. He was tall, not quite matching my height but around 6 foot I guessed.

We looked at each other for just a moment, and I moved forward and stuck out my hand to him. "Hi, I am Curtis. It's nice to meet you."

Kane took my hand but held onto a little longer that was polite business etiquette, as he looked me up and down. "Oh, you look less like a Mr Darcy than I thought you would, and more like a hip barista in a trendy London cafe. Or perhaps a trendy chef, given you are in a kitchen currently. Also hello, lovely to meet you too."

Kane dropped his right hand and held out the bottle of red wine in his left. "And second also, I bought wine, because Lucy is not a wine person and I need a decent drink to get through the meet the new boyfriend routine. Shall we drink wine together, Mr Darcy?"

"Absolutely," I responded.

Seated around the kitchen table a little while later, I was full and happy. I could tell both Kane and Lucy had a bit of a buzz from the wine, and I purposefully matched their relaxed manner. As we ate, I asked Kane some questions about his work, and with Lucy's help skilfully avoided providing too much detail about my own career. Kane's passion for the community supermarkets he was establishing across the country was evident in every word he said. A few of the stories he told about the people who had come into a Kane's looking for a warm meal and some support were a little heartbreaking.

"That was a magnificent meal, thank you Curtis." Kane said as he placed his knife and fork together purposefully on his plate. "Lucy, you have done well."

"But tell me Curtis, there are two more things I need to know about you," Kane continued. "Firstly, how did you learn to cook such good Greek food?"

That was an easy question and I didn't even have to mould my answer. "Well, I spent about a year working in Greece in my mid-twenties. After university I worked in an office for a while, and hated every moment of it, so I took off to a Greek island and worked on a fishing boat. It gave me some time to reflect about what I wanted to do with my life, and also to learn how to cook the local food. I rented a room from an elderly couple, and did a lot to help around the house, in return for which I got cooking lessons."

Kane was nodding thoughtfully along as I spoke. "Excellent, excellent."

Lucy was watching me intently as I explained this, a small smile on her face. I had not yet told her this part of my history, so the story was new to her as well. "I didn't know that," she said. "That must have been interesting."

"It was. I was in my rebellious phase and my parents

and some other significant people in my life were all trying to control how I lived my life. My parents, who are very wonderful, and I love very much just for the record, were keen for me to settle down and have a very boring under the radar life. I thought that was a waste, and when we clashed about it, I went travelling for a while. To find myself I suppose. It worked too, I found myself and as a bonus I now know how to fish and how to cook."

"Anyway, you said there were two things, Kane. What else can I tell you about myself?" I hoped this was something that I could answer.

"Well, I was going to ask you, Mr Darcy the dashing Englishman, whether there is also a Mr what-his-name in your story? You know the friend of Mr Darcy that ends up with the sister?" Kane laughed and turned to Lucy for assistance. "Lucia, you have a photographic memory, you must know the name of Mr Darcy's friend in Pride and Prejudice?"

"Mr Bingley," Lucy supplied dryly.

"Yes Mr Bingley. That's it! Is there any Mr Bingley in your life who might be interested in an American shopkeeper like me? So we can all go on picnics together and eat tiny sandwiches and play croquet in the gardens and such."

"Kane, you do realise it's the 21st century now, right? I don't think anyone plays croquet anymore and Curtis' family is not landed gentry with a giant house in the country." Lucy was struggling to keep a straight face. "And it is a truth universally acknowledged that I do not like sandwiches, tiny or otherwise."

"Yes, that's very true. Sorry to disappoint, but I have never played croquet in my life," I said. "My parents do have a house in the country, sort of, but it is a regular family home in a village not far outside London, not a sprawling estate with gardens and sheep and stuff."

Kane sighed. "Oh well, worth a try I suppose, but if you come across any Mr Bingleys, please let me know Curtis. I do like the croquet and picnics idea though."

Lucy had picked up her phone and was rapidly typing. I knew her well enough now to know that was her 'must research the idea I just had' look. When she finished typing and reading, she smiled. "There is a croquet club right here in New York. In Central Park. You could join Kane and learn to play in your spare time."

"Yes, *all* my spare time. When I am not running a major retail business, I will get right on with that. Anyway, enough of that fantasy. Let's talk more about your trip to London Lucy, I still don't have all the gossip."

As Lucy and Kane talked about her time at the conference in Oxford and then our time together in London, I reflected that I did in fact know someone who would fit the description of Kane's Mr Bingley. Tory's family did have a large family estate in the country, with the required gardens for playing croquet and I was pretty sure also some sheep. Tory was very discreet about his background, however, and would not want me talking about it. I knew about keeping secrets, so I was happy to honour his.

By the end of the night, I felt that I had passed the 'best friend' test with Kane. I had not got a call out for any sort of emergency and Kane had liked my cooking. Kane had been an important part of Lucy's life for a long time now, and when they were together, I could feel the deep affection and respect he and Lucy had for each other. I hoped that my relationship with Lucy would not impact on that in any way.

Kane left about 11pm, claiming to have a busy day

tomorrow. The kitchen was a bit of a mess, as I had never been good at cleaning as I go when I cooked, but it wouldn't take me long to get it clean. Lucy was tired, and I sent her off to get ready for bed while I washed and tidied.

———

Once Lucy had gone to bed and the kitchen was clean, I made myself a cup of tea and sat out on the back terrace in the night air listening to the sounds of the city. It was cooler now, but the air was still warm and humid. I really liked Lucy's brownstone, and it was very comfortable here. While I could leave Lucy sleeping and go anywhere in the world without her even noticing, the fact that I was officially in New York this weekend made me feel like I should stay in the house overnight if no emergencies cropped up.

We had only known each other a short while, but I knew I was in love with Lucy. It was very wonderful that she seemed to be my person. This weekend had been a taste of what regular life could be together, shopping, talking, laughing and dealing with everyday domestic issues. It made me realise that I needed to take some serious steps to restructure my life.

The first step would be for me to move to New York. Even though I easily commute from my place to hers in only a few minutes, it wasn't the same when there was an ocean between us. Technically I was entering the country illegally every time I visited Lucy, flying in without going through immigration. Cyran the superhero alien could get away with that, as certainly no one was going to try and arrest me when I was working. But to live with Lucy, regular boring old Curtis Harrington needed to be able to live in the US, and that was going to be more complicated.

As I drank my tea, I did some research on my phone on routes I could use get a green card and have the right to live and work here. The most straightforward would be to marry Lucy, and while I hoped that would be on the cards in the future, that was not something either of us were ready to talk about just yet. I didn't have any special skills or technical expertise that would warrant a work visa, (apart from the obvious), and holding down an actual job would be very complicated for me anyway.

Sitting here at Lucy's house in the middle of the night quietly planning was all well and good, but this was certainly something I should talk to Lucy about. We had not yet discussed the future, and I didn't know how fast Lucy wanted to move in our relationship.

What I did know was that both of us, and particularly Lucy, would be very busy in the coming months with all the work created by the comet taskforce. With all of that coming up perhaps now was not the right time to be making big life decisions.

Chapter 18
Lucy

For the rest of July my focus was on working with the other scientists to finalise the three satellites we were sending into orbit, so they were ready to use against the comet if needed.

While the preparation and planning were happening in Washington, the construction work was being done in Florida. This meant I was sharing my time between three locations, usually flying to Washington on Sunday night and then down to Florida on Wednesday and home to New York on Friday evening. The commuting alone was exhausting. Thankfully I had no other significant work commitments that I needed to juggle on top of long days working with NASA, as it was summer break for the universities.

It was brutally hot and humid in both Florida and Washington, even by July standards. The east cost of the US and Canada was suffering under an extended heatwave. Construction sites were closed, trains were running slow, and tourists stumbled through the streets drenched in sweat while trying to enjoy their summer break.

There were concerns about vulnerable people who did

not have access to air-conditioning being at high risk. Kane had instructed his team to ensure that all Kane's Community Marts were open 24 hours a day for anyone who wanted a place to shelter out of the heat, and our stores were providing free bottled water and ice pops to anyone, kid or adult, who wanted one.

I was disappointed I was not spending much time with Kane, as I had temporarily stopped doing my regular Wednesday morning visits to company headquarters, and I was much too tired to socialise when I was home on the weekends in New York. We were keeping in touch mostly through texting, with Kane keen for updates on any developments in my relationship with Cyran.

There was actually not a lot for me to report to Kane. It had been wonderful spending so much time with Cyran over the Fourth of July weekend. I felt that we had faced a couple of important tests in our relationship that weekend, and both had gone very well. We had proved we could cohabitate successfully and were very compatible in other intimate ways.

It was obvious to me that I was getting very close to being in love with Cyran. Attraction for me was about emotional intimacy first and foremost, and I was developing a deep connection with him. But our relationship was still very new. We had not yet talked about any next steps, however in my quiet moments in airports or between meetings I was doing some thinking about the implications of being with someone was not only an alien and a superhero but who lived in a different country to me.

I was getting used to Cyran working as a superhero and adapting to him switching between his two identities. When we were together, Cyran and Curtis were the same person, and that was the one that I was falling in love with.

Cleo Burwood

My taskforce work with NASA was challenging and interesting, but I deeply resented the fact that it meant Cyran and I were spending so much time apart while I commuted up and down the East Coast. I wanted to spend my time this summer building our relationship not building rockets.

It was not like Cyran was sitting around at home waiting for me. The combination of the heatwave in the US and Canada and millions of people being on vacation across Europe and North America meant a range of minor and some major emergencies that kept Cyran very busy. He had also spent nearly a week in Oregon helping with wildfires and a several days Yemen after a minor earthquake.

Cyran was very wary of coming to visit me when I was away from home on taskforce business, as he had to be careful about being spotted by people who knew him. Most of the taskforce members I was actively working with were staying in the same hotels as me, and Cyran did not want to be in a situation where he bumped into anyone, or where I potentially had to introduce my boyfriend Curtis to them. I respected the fact that Cyran tried to minimise the number of people who knew him as both Cyran and Curtis even though that meant us spending less time together.

We caught up mostly on Saturdays when I was in New York. Other nights we often spoke on the phone, unless Cyran was in the middle of something work related. One Thursday evening in late July Cyran and I managed a late-night phone call. It was technically the middle of the night for Cyran, as he was at his flat in London, but with the weird hours he kept that did not matter. I was in my hotel room in Florida, sitting in an armchair by the window with a view across the river towards the lights of the space centre.

As we chatted, Cyran casually mentioned that he had

been to Australia that morning and was surprised about how warm it was even through it was winter in the Southern Hemisphere. I was starting to get used to Cyran's days being a lot stranger than mine. His workplace stories were a quite different from most people's, not the average 'you won't believe what Fred in accounting said.'

"Where exactly were you and what hero stuff did you get up to down under?" I queried.

"I was in place called South Australia. Lots of wine grown in the area by the look of it. As I flew over, I could see miles and miles of vineyards."

"Sounds lovely," I commented. "But presumably something was going wrong?"

"Yes, there is a ferry service out to a big island off the coast, and one of the ferries got in trouble after a collision with a fishing trawler and started taking on water. I think they may have been fine without me, but I helped them out and pushed the ferry back to its mainland port."

A flash of envy that Cyran had got to spend time in Australia passed through me. Three years ago, I had been to Sydney for two days for a conference and meeting. I had seen the Sydney Harbour Bridge and the Opera House, as both were visible from the window of my hotel room, but I had not done anything touristy. I had been keen ever since to see more of the country.

"I am bit jealous that you got to go to Australia, even for work," I admitted. "It has been on my bucket list for a long time to spend some time more there."

"Well, perhaps when all this crazy comet stuff is over, we could go on a holiday there together?" Cyran suggested casually.

"Yes, absolutely!" I hoped Cyran could hear the enthusiasm I was feeling. "I have really only been there for work, and I would love to do a trip to Australia. We could do the Great Barrier Reef, and Sydney, and see the kangaroos and quokkas."

"Quokkas?" Cyran sounded slightly confused.

"Yes, you know quokkas, the little smiley animals that are famous on social media and people want to take selfies with them? We must visit them too. I'm sure the quokkas would like you, particularly as you are social media famous too," I said jokingly.

"Ok, I will have to look that up. I have been to Australia several times, often to help with bushfires or cyclones, but never relaxed or properly seen any of the sights. Or any quokkas I don't think." Cyran paused for a moment, obviously thinking, and then continued, "You said you had been there already?"

"I have just seen the Sydney Opera House and the Harbour Bridge. That's pretty much it. Except of course for the inside of the convention centre, which was nice but pretty standard really."

"Then a holiday to Australia sounds like a great idea. As I am self-employed, or possibly unemployed depending on how you look at it, I can be free pretty much anytime that suits you," Cyran said. "With the proviso that I will need to keep my work phone on and might need to disappear if there is a disaster happening somewhere."

"Of course," I replied. "I have accepted that is pretty much going to be standard for doing anything with you. I am going to have to get used to you being late, and not showing up for things, with me having to make excuses and lie to the people around me about where you are." I was tired so perhaps my tone was a bit sharper than it should have been.

Cyran was quiet for a moment, and then when he spoke

his voice was subdued. "Sorry about that. I understand it is difficult."

"Don't be sorry, I am not trying to make you feel bad." Realising I perhaps had been a bit too blunt, I tried to sound reassuring. "It's just the opposite really, I was trying to tell you that I understand the implications of being your partner and what it is going to involve for us to have a relationship. And that I am 100 percent okay with that."

"Thank you, I appreciate that, but this is a bit deep for over the phone. Can we go back to talking about kangaroos?"

"Of course." Taking my cue from Cyran, I was happy to change the subject back to our fantasy holiday in Australia.

"You could fly out to Sydney, and I could meet you there. I think you would probably have to go via LA, you may know as you have done the trip before," Cyran said.

"Or we could fly out together like regular people," I suggested. "It is long, about fifteen hours from LA to Sydney, but we can go first class which is reasonably comfortable. Or I could charter a plane which would be even better."

"Umm, so about that. This is possibly the strangest thing you will ever hear me say, but I am not that fond of flying. Or more to the point, fond of planes. I feel very claustrophobic and these days I don't want to be unavailable for a long period of time in case anyone needs me. A plane at 30,000 feet is not the sort of place you can easily sneak out of."

"That is one of the stranger things you have said," I agreed. While Cyran's views made sense, I was not keen on the idea of having to fly alone to Australia, or anywhere else we wanted to go in the future.

"But on the other hand," Cyran pointed out, "I am very

handy to have along on a holiday, particularly if you forget anything. A couple of years ago we had a family holiday in Portugal with my sister, her twins and Mum and Dad, and I was constantly popping home to get extra stuff for the kids, and mum's phone charger etc etc."

It seemed that Cyran was a bit low vibe today and didn't want to talk about anything significant. Despite this, he had just given me an opening to discuss something that had been weighing on my mind, so I seized the opportunity.

"Speaking of your parents, I should come to London again sometime soon and meet them. If I can find a gap in the taskforce work, it will be no problem for me to jump on a plane and come across for a few days. I would like to spend some time in your part of the world, and meet them all, including Beth and the kids."

"Yeh, sure, that sounds alright at some point, but no rush." Cyran's response was non-committal.

"Okay," I said, unsure of how to respond to his lack of enthusiasm. "Just keep it in mind and let me know what suits you. I am sure your parents are keen to meet me though, so it would be really nice."

"Sure," Cyran said again, still sounding very low vibe. "Things are just really busy and complicated at the moment. Let's worry about family stuff after the comet task-force is finished. I don't want to make you too tired, so I will say good night now. Will talk to you again tomorrow night Dr Lucy."

Cyran's use of my nickname cheered me slightly as we said goodbye. His response when I mentioned meeting his parents had surprised me. I hoped there was not something weird going on in that space. Perhaps Cyran was right, and things were just too busy and complicated.

Chapter 19
Cyran

I felt terrible for days about how I had handled the phone call with Lucy. She had definitely picked up on my lukewarm response to the idea that she come to London to meet my parents. I also felt terrible about the underlying cause of my response, that being that I had still not worked up the courage to tell my parents about Lucy's existence. Unfortunately, I could not really explain to myself why this was the case, let alone try to explain it to Lucy.

My parents may not know about my relationship with Lucy, but friends Pete and Josh now did. A few days after he had been discharged from hospital, Pete, Tory and I had sat with Josh at his home and described all the details of the day, including how I had got him hospital so quick, and where I had been when I got Tory's urgent phone that day. Josh had been incredulous at first, assuming that we were pranking him and then very shocked that I had managed to keep my identity such a secret for many years.

Tory had recently started a new group chat for the four

of us, which he titled 'boys who know stuff' and all three of them seemed to delight in sending me memes about my superhero activities. It was wonderfully freeing to know that I had the support of my closest friends and could be honest with them about my work, and the logistics of my long-distance relationship with Lucy.

One Tuesday in early August the taskforce reconvened in Washington, and just before 10am both Lucy and I were once again in the NASA conference room waiting for the meeting to start. We had seen each other this morning in New York, before Lucy left for the airport. Once she was on her way, I left her house to fly home to London for a few hours before returning across the Atlantic for this meeting.

We had decided this time to not bother to hide from the other taskforce members that we were friendly. This morning we had planned what I was going to bring Lucy for lunch today, assuming we were still in the meeting by that point. If the meeting finished before lunchtime, we would get lunch somewhere here in the city before Lucy headed home.

When I arrived in the courtyard, Lucy was standing inside drinking from a large takeaway coffee cup. I entered the room, said hello to a few people, and then grabbed a bottle of water and wandered over to join her. "Hello Dr Lucy. What have you been up to since I last saw you?" I asked playfully.

"Hello. I am good, in fact not much different to last time you saw me. My flight down from New York this morning was fine and totally routine." Lucy took a sip of her coffee.

"Mine too, although I did go via London for a couple of hours which made it a bit longer."

"Did you do anything exciting with your time at home?" Lucy asked me.

"Not really. The main thing I did was some grocery shopping. I have not been home much lately, and there was very little in my fridge." I didn't want to explain to Lucy that now when I was at home in London, the flat felt a little cold and lonely, as I was sending most of my spare time in New York.

The main door to the room opened at that point and Director Malone came in accompanied by three people who had not been to the previous taskforce sessions.

"I will talk to you later," I whispered to Lucy. "Have fun." She smiled at me and walked around the room to her seat.

"Thank you to everyone for gathering today," Director Malone said once we had all sat down. "I acknowledge those of you who have travelled again to be here, and our overseas participants joining us online." She smiled as she continued, "I have some very good news to share. It is now confirmed that the comet will have a very near miss with the Earth, and we will not need to take action to stop it impacting us."

There was some spontaneous applause. Everyone around the room looked very relieved.

The Director then continued, "I am thrilled about this outcome, as I am sure you all are too. Unfortunately, there is still some work and planning we need to do today. Firstly, we need to decide whether to proceed with finishing the satellites, and secondly, we need to plan for telling the public about the comet. As you all know, the original directive from President Clifton was that the news would not be revealed until there was a definitive answer about the comet's trajectory. Now that this issue had been resolved we need to start planning in detail."

Gesturing to the three people who had come into the room with her, Director Malone explained, "These are my colleagues from the NASA communications team, and are here to lead a discussion about the best messaging. They will lead the development of a communications strategy, but I am keen for any input today on the most effective way to present the science around the comet."

After much discussion, the taskforce made the decision to continue work on the satellites and still send them into orbit, but with a payload of cameras and other data gathering devices to study the comet up close rather than try to break it up. The other major topic for the taskforce meeting was how and when to tell the world about the comet.

Two weeks later Director Malone and I stood beside President Clifton as she held a press conference in the gardens of the White House on a very hot Wednesday morning. The sun was beating down on us as we fronted a large gaggle of journalists. Over the next few hours many of the other world leaders would hold their own press events, telling their people in their own languages about what to expect.

The President announced to the assembled media, and the world beyond, that the Earth was very shortly going to be passing through the tail of the Mauna Kea comet, with it being only a few weeks until it would be visible to the naked eye across the globe. The messaging stressed that there was no need for public concern, with the only consequence of the comet likely to be some potential disruption to communication networks. The comet's arrival was promoted as a once in a lifetime opportunity to witness an amazing celestial event.

Following the announcement, however, the world's media and social media went into meltdown. The day after the announcement resulted in the highest volume of social media traffic ever recorded and #comet was majorly trending. Unfortunately, #Cyranwillsavesus was trending as well. No pressure at all there.

Two days after the comet announcement, I started work on a communications tour being managed by the United Nations. The Secretary General, an international contingent of scientists, and myself were to go travelling the globe to provide information and reassurance. The plan was to hold media events and community information sessions across 80 countries and dozens of languages over a two-week period. The message was always the same no matter what the language, that the sky will be look weird for a few weeks, but there was no need for the public to panic.

While I was part of the tour contingent, I was not travelling with the group. I could leave them once we were finished at each location and then meet up with them at the next. As a result, I managed some large blocks of free time while the group was either on a plane or getting some sleep in a hotel in whatever city was on the itinerary for that day.

Some of this downtime was spent doing my normal job helping with of everyday emergencies, and some with Lucy when we were lucky enough to both have free time. With the rapidly approaching deadline for the launch of the satellites in early September, however, there unfortunately was not much time when Lucy was home and wasn't working.

By the last weekend in August my communications tour was finally over. Lucy and I had plans to spend that weekend together in New York, starting with going out together for a proper date at a nice restaurant on Friday night. Once again, our plans were disrupted, as I got called out to help with a typhoon in the South China Sea making landfall in the Philippines. I spent all day and much of Friday night assisting with evacuating people out of flood waters and doing search and rescue. By the time I arrived in New York it was quite late and we had definitely missed our reservation for dinner.

When I got to Lucy's house, I let myself in quietly from the back terrace. I found Lucy curled up on the couch in her living area with the TV on in the background while she read a book. The evidence of the white boxes on the coffee table showed she had long since ordered Chinese takeaway.

"Hello, you stink," she said honestly as I bent down to kiss her in greeting. "Go and have a shower before you come anywhere near me, please. There's plenty of food when you are clean and ready." So much for a romantic evening.

Ten minutes later I was back downstairs. I had washed off the remnants of mud and flood waters and hopefully smelled much better now. Lucy had migrated to the kitchen and had microwaved the takeaway containers and spread them out on the kitchen island bench. The island bench was a cozy space to one side of the room designed for very casual eating, with six high stools spread around a white marble bench top that matched the rest of the kitchen. I had not actually measured it, but I was pretty sure that the island bench was bigger than my whole kitchen at home in London.

The takeaway looked and smelled very enticing. Not surprisingly, I was starving and so I was not shy about jumping straight into the food. Lucy sat across from me, chopsticks in her hand, picking at bits and pieces of the food as we talked, listening to me vent about the day.

"Today just sucked," I told her honestly. "I know I see people all the time in this job who are having the worst days of their lives, but I find it especially hard when I help people who are already just getting by. It is not fair that they now have to deal with something like today's typhoon. The injustice of that just gets at me."

Lucy nodded, recognising that I didn't need suggestions or solutions, just a supportive ear.

"I know that overall, I am doing what I want to with my life. I get to use my abilities and be who I really am by helping people from all over the world, but it is just extremely hard sometimes. I love you, I love our life together, and logically I know I should not feel guilty about coming back here to this ridiculous awesome house or my lovely little flat in London after working hard to help, but I do sometimes."

Lucy had developed a strange look on her face as I was talking, and she seemed slightly lost for words when I was finished. It went on long enough that I was mildly concerned.

"Are you okay? What's going on?" I asked her, putting down my chopsticks and looking intently at her.

She reached forward and grabbed my hand with a smile. "I am absolutely fantastic, thank you. Do you realise you just told me you love me for the first time in the middle of all that venting?"

"Oh." I was shocked to realise that was in fact what I had just said. Of course, I was not shocked that I loved

Lucy, as I think I had known that for many weeks now, even if I hadn't yet verbalised it. "Sorry, that wasn't very romantic, was it?"

"Please don't be sorry," Lucy reassured me. "Overall, it works out quite well really, given I love you too."

Chapter 20
Lucy

S aturday was a sleep-in day for me. Cyran still hadn't yet figured out the complexities of my espresso machine, so once I was finally awake, he ducked out to my local café for a couple of takeaways and some pastries for breakfast.

It was a lovely morning, with the expected heat of the day not yet here, so I roused myself out of bed when Cyran returned with coffee and joined him on the terrace outside the kitchen. The terrace, which was on the roof of the lowest floor of the brownstone, gave me about 25 square feet of outdoor living space. That was enough room for a small outdoor dining table and two couches facing each other. The floor was limestone pavers and there was a crisp line of neatly trimmed bamboo plants around the outside of the space, creating a green barrier and privacy from the neighbours.

Cyran and I were both expected in Florida on Monday morning for the launch of the satellites that were now structured to observe the comet rather than break it apart. I was leaving New York Sunday afternoon to fly down to the space centre, but until then our weekend was completely free. It was a lovely feeling that there was nothing I needed to do and nowhere anyone expected me to be, if only for a brief window of 36 hours.

"How are you feeling about the launch on Monday?" Cyran asked me as we drank our coffees. "Are you looking forward to the project being over?"

"I am not feeling particularly nervous about how it will all go on Monday. We have now done everything we possibly can to make it a success. And I am very definitely looking forward to the launch and the whole taskforce project being over. I am really tired of all the commuting back and forth and want everything in my life to go back to normal. Although I suppose it will be a new normal now that we are together."

"Yes, you are right, it will be a new normal," Cyran agreed. "Our relationship is by far the best thing to come out of the whole taskforce situation and I looking forward to spending some more time together once this is all over."

"And also having the chance for a break from work would be nice too. I missed a chance to have a break this summer, so perhaps we can away together in the next few weeks for a vacation, possibly even our Australia trip, although that is a long way to go for a short trip," I suggested.

"Sounds lovely."

"Do you have any suggestions for somewhere relatively local that would be good for a holiday in next few weeks?" I asked Cyran. "Perhaps somewhere that looked nice when you there helping with a crisis?"

Cyran suddenly seemed a little uncomfortable. "Umm not sure. A holiday sounds good. I will have to think about where to go and also think about timing stuff around when I am free."

"Oh, have you got a packed schedule coming up that I don't know about?" I asked jokingly.

"Not for the next week or so, as obviously I have kept that free for comet stuff. The weekend after that I have a thing to go to in London. It's my cousin's engagement party, so I need to make an appearance for family sake. I suppose even if we were away, it wouldn't be a problem to leave you to read a book for a few hours and head to London for the party."

I sucked in a breath, completely shocked and horrified by what Cyran had just said. I pushed away from the table, stood up and took a few steps towards the back of the garden, turning my back on Cyran for just a moment. When I turned back to face him, Cyran was looking at me with a slightly puzzled expression. "What's going on Lucy? Are you okay?" he asked.

"No," I snapped at him. "Of course I am not okay. Were you really going to go to a party with your family and not invite me? Do you realise how awful that makes me feel?"

Cyran was quiet.

Tears were starting to fight their way out of my eyes, and I wiped them away with the back of my hand. I didn't want to cry yet as I was still busy being angry. "You have been putting off introducing me to your parents, and now that this perfect opportunity for me to meet your family comes up, you don't even mention it to me. Are you embarrassed by me? Or is it that you want me to be Cyran's girlfriend but not Curtis's?"

Cyran found his voice. He spoke quietly, his tone a bit defensive but not angry. "No, that's not it, Lucy. I just didn't think of it like that. Of course I am not embarrassed by you."

"It's complicated," he continued, dropping his head forward and resting it in his hands, "with you being an American, and Dad having such close ties to the Government still, and my parents not being particularly supportive of me being a superhero, so I didn't want to make you uncomfortable. I thought of it as saving you from a difficult social situation."

"I don't need saving Cyran," I said firmly. "You might spend your life saving strangers, but don't patronise me please by thinking you need to save me too. You should have talked to me about this."

"Yes, I know that now. I am sorry." Cyran continued to not look at me.

"I love you Cyran, but right now I don't like you very much. Can you go home please and just give me some space? I am disappointed and hurt and I need some alone time to process my emotions."

Cyran looked up at me across the table. I could see his face again and he too was fighting back tears. "Sure, I will just get changed upstairs and head back London."

He stood up slowly, perhaps waiting for me to say something reassuring, or that he should stay. Unfortunately, I didn't feel capable of that just yet. Still angry, I just stood there and let him go.

About half an hour later I managed to get up and take the remains of coffee and breakfast inside to the kitchen. I had not seen Cyran leave, so he had either left on foot through the front door or flown away from the house via the small Juliet balcony off my bedroom. My anger with Cyran had swiftly turned to tears once he was gone, and I had just finished a bout of undignified sobbing.

Needing some emotional support, I found my phone in the kitchen and called Kane, hoping he could come over and help me process what had just happened with Cyran. When the call connected it was obviously Kane was somewhere out in public rather than at home, as there was a great deal of background noise.

"Hey Kane. Are you free at all today to come over and eat junk food with me?" I asked. "Curtis and I have just had our first real fight, and it was a big one. I need someone to debrief and eat ice cream with."

"Oh no, that sounds awful. Of course I can come over. Whatever you need Lucy." Kane's response was understanding and empathetic. "I am currently at the gym and was just about to take a spin class, but I can ditch that and come straight to you if you need me. Otherwise, I will come in about an hour after my class, and after a shower of course."

"Thank you. After your class is soon enough. That would be awesome. I need to have a shower and wash my face from all the crying anyway. I will organise an indulgent lunch and some ice cream delivery."

"Cool, I will sweat first, then be with you as soon as I can. It will all be okay Lucy, just hang in there sweetie."

Kane was still here around lunchtime when a ridiculously large bunch of flowers was delivered to my brownstone. The card with the flowers simply read, "*Sorry I am an idiot. I love you. Cxx*"

When he had first arrived, Kane and I had thoroughly debriefed about my argument with Cyran. Lots of ice cream helped. A few hours later I felt that I had experienced every emotional response possible to the fight and the whole situation with Cyran's parents, and I was now feeling sad rather than angry.

Talking it through, I realised that a lot of my sadness was coming from the fact that I felt like I had lost my perfect relationship with Cyran. Not necessarily that the relationship was over, as I was determined to salvage this and move on, but rather because our love for each other was not 'out of the box' shiny and unblemished anymore. It was a bit like the first time you scratched or dented a new car, or a new smartphone. It still worked fine but would never quite be the same again.

When I explained this thought to Kane, his wisdom was that the minor imperfections were what made any relationship much more real.

By Monday morning, Cyran and I still hadn't spoken to each other about what had happened in the garden on Saturday morning. As I requested, he had given me lots of space and hadn't called me, but he had texted several times to apologise on Saturday and Sunday and let me know he would come over immediately if I did want to talk.

By Sunday night I had finally decided I was ready to talk to Cyran. I wanted to accept his apology, tell him I loved him and then work with him on a plan for telling his parents about our relationship.

I had spent the flight from New York to Florida thinking again about the whole situation. I had realised that the engagement party next weekend didn't matter in the overall scheme of things. I wanted to be in this relationship long term and there would be many other opportunities to meet his extended family. What did matter though was meeting

Cyran's parents and I was not prepared to compromise on Cyran keeping us, or me, a secret from them.

It was nearly 9pm by the time I arrived in my hotel in Titusville after a 90-minute delay leaving New York. When I called Cyran once I had arrived and settled in, the call went to his voice mail. I hoped that no response meant he was out working rather than avoiding my call. I left a message just saying that I wanted to talk to him when we could get a chance. Looking for news of Cyran, I flicked through the television news channels until I saw footage of him in Japan. I left the TV on with the sound turned down as I went to sleep so I could at least have video of Cyran in my room with me that night.

On launch day itself there was nothing I specifically needed to do, other than be on site in case there was a problem with the battery packs in the satellites. The plan was for the three satellites to launch over a period of four hours starting mid-morning, so I was anticipating there was going to be a great deal of sitting or standing around waiting for things to happen.

Once the satellites were all in place, Cyran then had an important job to do. He was going to fly into orbit to check each one was operational and aligned correctly for optimal gathering of footage and data from the comet. The checking work Cyran was doing could have been done by remote control from the ground with more time to work on the control systems and software coding, but the speed at which we had needed to build the satellites meant it was quicker and easier to rely on Cyran's skills for this crucial step.

Cyran was also needed here as Director Malone had

specifically requested his presence to reassure the public, particularly as #cyranwillsaveus was still trending. He had quietly stood by the Director's side this morning as she had held an early morning press conference with the launch pad as a backdrop.

Cyran had not responded to my late-night voice mail message, but I knew that he had been working in Japan right up until a few minutes before the Director's press conference. I had overheard the concerns amongst the NASA press office staff about whether he was going to make it in time.

The first launch went very smoothly, the crowds both inside and outside the building cheering as the rocket took to the skies. Summer was over and school had started back last week, but it seemed that half of Florida had ditched school and work for the day to watch the launches.

It was very crowded in the flight control room, with people standing around observing as the teams behind the long panel of desks went about their work. There was also TV cameras in the room, broadcasting the launch across the world. I was keen to stay out of shot, so I hugged the sides of the room, and the TV cameras meant that there was definitely no opportunity for me to have a private conversation with Cyran.

After the first launch, I noticed Cyran had disappeared, probably to go home and get some food. He was back a couple of hours later in time for the second launch and stayed in the room until the third satellite launched successfully mid-afternoon.

Cyran did several TV interviews during quieter periods between the launches, discussing his role in the taskforce project and explaining what he was going to do when he went into orbit to check the satellites.

Coffee with a Superhero

We had spent so much time together that it now seemed odd to see him in work mode playing the slightly aloof alien. I stood at the side of the room with a coffee in my hand and watched him. Now that I knew the man behind the superhero mask, I could see that he looked tired and a little strained with just a tight professional smile in place as he spoke to the reporters. I knew he had been in Japan all of last night, and the last few days had been very stressful, so I was worried about when he had last managed to get some rest.

Shortly after the third rocket had successfully launched it was time for Cyran to head into low earth orbit to check the satellites. Cyran could hold his breath for about fifteen minutes, so the plan was that he could work in orbit in ten minute blocks and then fly back into breathable atmosphere for a few minutes. He was carrying a radio and would report in briefly each time.

Cyran's work on the first satellite, in orbit over the South Pacific, and second satellite over the North Atlantic was slow, taking about an hour each, but textbook perfect. Unfortunately, the same was not true for the final satellite over the northern Indian Ocean.

All went smoothly for the first few minutes. Then fifteen minutes went by with no communications, then the silence just keeping building to 30 minutes and then more than an hour. The Flight Director was keen that no-one panic, stressing that Cyran's radio could just be broken and he could still be working even if he was not able to make contact.

That hour of not knowing where Cyran was a horrendous experience. I was very worried that he was injured, hurt and alone, or worse, that he would never come back. What if we never had the chance to make peace after our argument on Saturday? Being in a very public place feeling all these emotions was awful, and I wanted to go home and hide and pretend none of this was happening.

But standing here I realised that now home for me was not just a place, but also a person. Cyran and the life we were building together was the home and the future I wanted. Now I just needed Cyran to come back so we could kiss and make up and get on with living our lives together.

Desperate for distraction, I went looking for another coffee. It was not like I needed any more caffeine, but it gave me something to do with my hands as I stood around worrying about Cyran. As I crossed the room my phone rang. It was an unknown number, the screen telling me the call was from Indonesia. I swiped to answer and put my phone my ear, answering with a simple Hello. What followed was the sweetest three words I had ever heard, "Hello Dr Lucy."

Epilogue
Lucy - Three months later

I stood in my kitchen looking at the giant mess left after Thanksgiving dinner and felt blissfully happy. Today had been wonderful. Cyran and I had hosted our first celebration here in New York in what was now our home, not just mine, as he had officially moved in with me earlier this month.

After our work with the comet taskforce was finally over, Cyran and I had slowly started the work of building a proper life together. The comet had passed through without any significant impacts and by early October it was all over. Some disruption to live-to-air television broadcasting had been the most significant consequence.

Cyran had lost contact with us on launch day because a piece of untracked Soviet era space junk had slammed into him while he was checking the satellites, knocking him out of orbit and spiralling fast towards the ground. He had lost his phone and radio when his flight suit ripped and lost consciousness when he hit the ground in Indonesia. Thankfully, a family of local farmers had helped him after he had crashed into their soybean field, provided the phone so he could ring me and then hosted Cyran for a few hours until he felt able to fly back to Florida.

Strangely, Cyran had got much of the public credit for the success of comet mission, even though it had been the taskforce members who had done the work developing the response plan and building the satellites. Our work had been formally recognised, however, with President Clifton hosting a reception for us all in the White House a few weeks ago. Cyran only attended very briefly, making an appearance for the sake of politeness, but not wanting to distract attention away from the hard-working scientists and engineers.

With some high-level help, Cyran now had a green card. President Clifton had been very happy to help any way she could, and all the paperwork to get Curtis Harrington the right to live and work in the US had been sorted quickly. I was sure the President was pleased to now have Cyran living in the country.

We had gathered many of the important people in our lives together today. My family were all here, including my brothers and sister, and the house had been full of kids' noise and laughter. The fact that Cyran had moved his gaming consoles from London, and with the addition of a new massive tv, had turned my former study off the living room into a gaming room had been a huge hit today with the younger generation. Last week we had also bought a foosball table and shopping trolley full of toys to help entertain my nieces and nephews.

Of course, Cyran's family were also very important to us. In the end I had gone with Cyran to his cousin's engagement party in September, the one that had caused all the conflict between us. I had flown into London two days beforehand, and Cyran and I had caught the train up to the village of High Wycombe to meet his parents, John and Helena, and his sister Beth and her twins in their hometown before the party.

Despite Cyran's concerns about how his parents would react to my existence, they had been extremely welcoming. Helena in particular had been very excited about the idea of Cyran having a girlfriend. I got the sense from a few comments she made that she had been worried for a while about whether his lifestyle would make it impossible to find someone to share his life with. Cyran loved playing with Beth's kids, and he was roped into some serious backyard soccer (sorry football!) matches with Ollie and Georgia after school. Helena and I had some long chats while sitting on the patio drinking tea and watching them all play. We were heading back to the UK for Christmas, and I was looking forward to the opportunity to know them all better.

The engagement party itself had been a whirlwind of being introduced to Cyran's relatives, repeating over and over the story of how Curtis and I had met when he was in the US on a work trip, and how he was now planning to move to New York. His cousin Rebecca seemed blissfully happy with her new fiancé Rishi, and we would no doubt be back London for a wedding in due course, probably next summer.

We had also taken a brief vacation while we were in the UK. It wasn't quite the tropical beach vacation I had originally envisaged but instead it was a week in an amazingly picturesque village by the sea in Cornwall. We rented a house with views of the ocean, and Cyran and I spent our day taking long walks, having relaxed meals in the local pub and reconnecting with each other after the intensity of the taskforce project and the drama between us about the engagement party. We had also taken the time to have some serious conversations about communicating better and established yet more parameters for how our life together was going to work.

When I returned to New York, the university semester was in full swing, and my work routine returned to its pre-taskforce normal. Currently I was still spending Thursday nights in Boston but was looking at whether I could reorganise my time so that would no longer be necessary. Although it wasn't a huge hardship being away from home when my boyfriend could fly into join me for dinner wherever I happened to be.

It had been a period of adjustment for both of us living together over the past few weeks, particularly as Cyran had such a random work schedule and usually needed only a few hours' sleep a night. I had been very happy to move my study upstairs so Cyran could have more space on the main living floor of the brownstone. We had filled the living spaces with things to keep him occupied both during the day and while I slept at night, including the new games room, and a small yoga studio and his own study in the basement.

Cyran had kept his flat in London, so we had a base on that side of the Atlantic. This made it much easier for Cyran when he flew across to see his family or his friends. We had also talked about buying a house in the town where his parents and sister lived to give us the privacy of our own place when we visited them. Our plan was to do some house hunting when we were there at Christmas.

The trip to Australia that Cyran and I had fantasised about back in July had not yet happened but was still very much part of the future we were planning together. Neither of us felt there was any rush. The current tentative plan was to go in March, when it was spring break for me here, and hopefully good weather in Australia once the blistering heat of their summer was over.

The degree of mess I was current looking at in the kitchen was witness to the number of people we had gathered in the house today. There had been the 19 of us in the Cortez family including Cyran, and we had also had both Kane and Tory with us today. Kane was a standard part of a Cortez family Thanksgiving, and he had been joining us each year since we were in college. Kane's relationship with his own family was very strained, and he felt more welcome here with us than going home to Michigan.

It had been a pleasant surprise for Cyran when Tory asked him a few weeks back if he could come to New York and stay with us for Thanksgiving. As Englishmen, Cyran and Tory had never celebrated Thanksgiving, so we had great fun today explaining the traditions and watching for reactions as they ate cornbread and pumpkin pie for the first time.

Over lunch Tory had been interrogated by my sister Gabriela for stories of embarrassing things he and Cyran had got up to at school and university. Thankfully there were kids in the room, so the stories were pretty tame.

Needing an excuse for a break from work, Tory had flown in Tuesday and was staying through to Sunday morning. Tory was a well-mannered house guest, and the fact that he knew Cyran's secret identity meant that we could all relax. Now that the formal part of the Thanksgiving celebrations was over, Cyran and Tory were both looking forward to spending some time together in the coming days. I had organised tickets for them to the hockey game at Madison Square Garden on Friday night and we were going to take Tory to out to do several touristy things this weekend.

Right now, Tory was not in the house, as after my family had all left, Kane had somewhat surprisingly declared that the two of them were going for walk together to work off all the calories and people watch in Central Park. Kane had bundled Tory out the door, giving Cyran and I some much-needed time alone. It made me happy that our two best friends had seemed to get on very well today.

Life was really good.

Cyran came up behind me and wrapped his arms around my waist from behind, hugging me tight. He tipped his head and brushed his lips against my cheek.

"Well done today, Dr Lucy. That was a fabulous day. First and best Thanksgiving ever, thank you. I love you lots and lots."

I wriggled out of Cyran's grip and turn to face him, so we could look at each other. "I love you too, and I will love you even more if you help me clean all this mess," I teased. "Don't you dare think about suddenly having to go rescue a rhino or something, I need you here."

"No rhinos, I need to be here, this is where I belong." Cyran's voice was intense, he was being more serious than me. His eyes were practically glowing as he looked at me, full of emotion as we stood together in the middle of the kitchen.

"Yes, good. Please help me work out what to deal with next."

Cyran's hand reached up to cup my face gently. "Darling Dr Lucy, do not worry about what's next, it will all be fine," he said softly. "Let's tidy up the kitchen, I will make you a coffee and then when we are ready, let's get married."

And so we did.

Acknowledgments

Big thanks to my fabulous beta reader Liz, for your insightful comments on the manuscript, and to Andy for the cover design work.

Thank you also to my family, who provided me with the encouragement and support I needed to take the giant scary leap from being someone who always wanted to write a novel to someone who actually has!

About the Author

Cleo Burwood lives in Perth, Australia with a husband who loves aeroplanes and an aloof but adorable tuxedo cat.

Cleo has always had stories swirling around inside her head, and now that her kids have grown up and don't need her quite so much, she has found the time to give her characters the attention they deserve.

Coffee with a Superhero is her first novel.